'Forgive me.'

Jane gazed up into his eyes. For a moment she felt weak and vulnerable, close to the tears she had been suppressing.

George hesitated, then bent his head, his lips brushing her brow. The caress comforted her, though she ought to have rejected it. Instead she wanted to cling to him.

Jane felt his arms close about her. He held her next to his body and his lips touched her hair; he stroked the back of her neck with his fingertips, his warmth comforting her. He did nothing to indicate a desire to make love to her. His embrace was one of comfort and reassurance—nothing more.

For a moment Jane wished that she might stay in his arms for ever, but then she remembered who she was and why she was with this man and drew back…

SECRETS AND SCANDALS

*Nothing stays secret for long
in Regency Society!*

The truth threatens to
reveal a scandal for three couples
in this exciting new Regency trilogy from

Anne Herries

THE DISAPPEARING DUCHESS—
February 2012

THE MYSTERIOUS LORD MARLOWE—
March 2012

THE SCANDALOUS LORD LANCHESTER—
April 2012

**You can also find these as eBooks
at www.millsandboon.co.uk**

THE MYSTERIOUS LORD MARLOWE

Anne Herries

First published in Great Britain 2012
by Mills & Boon, an imprint of Harlequin (UK) Limited.
Large Print edition 2012
Harlequin (UK) Limited, Eton House, 18-24 Paradise Road, Richmond, Surrey TW9 1SR

© Anne Herries 2012

ISBN: 978 0 263 22518 1

00982853

Harlequin (UK) policy is to use papers that are natural, renewable and recyclable products and made from wood grown in sustainable forests. The logging and manufacturing process conform to the legal environmental regulations of the country of origin.

Printed and bound in Great Britain
by CPI Antony Rowe, Chippenham, Wiltshire

Anne Herries lives in Cambridgeshire, where she is fond of watching wildlife, and spoils the birds and squirrels that are frequent visitors to her garden. Anne loves to write about the beauty of nature, and sometimes puts a little into her books—although they are mostly about love and romance. She writes for her own enjoyment, and to give pleasure to her readers. She is a winner of the Romantic Novelists' Association Romance Prize. She invites readers to contact her on her website: www.lindasole.co.uk

Prologue

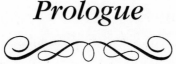

'That is my only offer. Take it or leave it.'

The tall gentleman looked into the face of the man who had spoken and knew him for a rogue. Blake was lying through his teeth and he would be a fool to believe one word the man said—and yet what could he do but agree to the devil's proposal?

'You are asking me to help you abduct a respectable young woman?' he asked because he needed to say the words aloud to get them clear in his mind. 'You refuse my money and demand that I go along with this outrageous affair in exchange for the return of my property—am I right?'

'The girl is willing enough. She wants it to look as if it is an abduction so that her guardian will not refuse our marriage. He holds the purse strings and will release her fortune to save her reputation.'

'I do not see why you need my help if the girl is willing to wed you?'

'I must be sure that no harm comes to her. The men I employ aren't of the best character and they might decide to carry her off themselves for the ransom. Her guardian hates me and if he guessed I was involved he would never release her fortune to me. Therefore I must employ someone I can trust—and if you wish to protect a certain lady's good name you will oblige me.'

'You swear to me that this young lady is willing?'

'I have said it,' Blake grunted and glared at him. 'Please yourself, sir. If you want those letters returned, then that is my price.'

Blake was in his late thirties, good-looking enough in his own way—apart from his odd eyes. Of differing shades, they gave him a strange appearance, which was slightly sinister.

'Then you leave me little choice. I do not see why you need my help, but if it is the only way...'

'You will speak to her, reassure her, stay with

her until I join you both at a place we shall agree upon. My men will do the business, but you must keep your word and stay with her until we meet.'

The tall gentleman frowned, certain now that Blake was lying about the girl's willingness to be abducted. His instincts told him to walk away. He should go to a magistrate and tell him what he knew—but if he did that someone he cared for would lose everything. He was caught between the devil and destruction. Besides, he did not even know the young woman's name; if he did not help Blake the abduction would still take place. Blake would find someone else to do his dirty work and then there would be no chance of thwarting him.

'Where will you be whilst this deed takes place?'

'I shall be nearby, watching you. My men shall take the young lady to a fresh carriage that I shall have waiting—you will accompany her until we get to the rendezvous point and then you will go your own way.'

'And then you will return my property?'

'You have my word on it.'

The word of a cheat and a liar. He did not for one moment believe that the girl was willing, but if he walked away now more than one lady might be ruined. If he agreed to this outrageous proposal, he might be able to spirit the lady away from under Blake's nose—and still get the letters that could ruin the good name of the sister he loved.

'Very well,' he said and offered his hand. 'I shall act as your go-between—and you will give me the letters?'

'Have I not given my word?'

'Renege on it and you will be sorry.' He looked at Blake, his gaze narrowed. 'When and where is this abduction to take place?'

Chapter One

'I have been dreading this visit,' Mariah, Lady Fanshawe, said and turned to look at her companion in the carriage, which was taking them to the house of her late husband's sister. 'I do not think I could have borne it had you not agreed to accompany me, Jane. Winston's family never approved of me, you know. His sister and Aunt Cynthia thought me too flighty—and accused me of marrying him simply for his fortune.'

'It is not like you to give way to a fit of nerves,' Jane Lanchester said, putting out a hand to touch her companion's hand. 'They cannot harm you, you know, Mariah. Winston left almost his entire fortune to you. His relatives may not like the situation, but they cannot change the will you told me that your husband went to some lengths to make certain you were protected.'

'The income is certainly mine, but the capital is tied up in a trust,' Mariah confided. 'I intended to ask Justin what I ought to do, but Lucinda has been a little unwell because of the baby. After all they've been through, I decided that it was best not to involve him in my affairs.'

Jane nodded, understanding perfectly. Justin, Duke of Avonlea, had been too worried about his wife, Lucinda, to become embroiled in Mariah's troubles, but it seemed that she was anxious about something and needed to open her heart to someone.

'You can tell me everything, you know,' Jane said. 'I am certain that my brother would do everything in his power to assist you were he here. Unfortunately, he was called suddenly to Paris on some business for the government.'

Mariah nodded, an odd look in her eyes. She had thought Lord Lanchester's visit to Paris might have been for another reason, but nothing had come of it. He remained there after Lucinda, the duke and Mariah had returned to England

and no doubt his sister knew more of his affairs than she.

She smothered a sigh. 'Andrew is a good friend, but he is suffering himself at the moment. You do know that he was very much in love with Lucinda Avonlea?'

'I know that Andrew found her charming and was concerned for her when she was embroiled in that unpleasant business of the blackmail,' Jane agreed. 'I also know that he admires you greatly, Mariah—particularly the way you handled yourself when that dreadful man tried to murder Lucinda.'

'Lord Lanchester is a decent and honourable man,' Mariah agreed, a little nerve flicking at her right temple. 'He is a good friend—but I am not sure that he could help with this problem.'

'Why do you not tell me? Perhaps a lawyer...'

Mariah hesitated. 'My husband's lawyer told me that the bulk of the fortune Winston left me is in the trust fund. I can draw the income, which is generous, and I have a small amount of capital—but the rest will not be released until I remarry. Winston thought I might fall prey to fortune hunters. The problem is that my trustees must approve my marriage.'

'Ah, I begin to see...' Jane saw her friend's mutinous look and smiled. 'You do not wish to be told whom you may marry by these trustees.'

'And they are Winston's sister, a querulous old woman, and her meddling husband,' Mariah said and pouted. 'My lawyer said that if the man I wished to marry was of good birth and above suspicion they could not withhold their consent, but why should I be beholden to them?'

'Surely they would not seek to interfere?' Jane asked, looking at her anxiously. Mariah was both brave and beautiful but she was also stubborn and at times contrary. 'Is there someone you would wish to marry?' she suggested gently.

'Well, I thought there might be, but—' Mariah broke off as they heard two shots followed by a scream, then the horses came to an abrupt halt and the two ladies were thrown into a heap on the floor of the carriage.

'Lawks a' mercy!' an uncultured voice exclaimed. 'There's two of 'em, guv. What do we do now?' Jane registered the fact that the man was pointing a wicked-looking pistol at them. He jerked it at them, indicating that they should step down from the carriage. 'Which one of yer is Mariah Fanshawe?'

Mariah was holding a kerchief to her forehead and appeared not to hear the question. Jane thought quickly. If she were not mistaken, this was an abduction. Mariah was an heiress and it was more than likely her fortune they were after than her.

'I am,' Jane said looking at Mariah. 'Say nothing, *Jane.* We are in some danger.'

'No...' Mariah had become aware of the situation. 'You can't...I shan't let you.'

Ignoring her, Jane got out of the carriage. There were four men, two of them had pistols trained on the coachman and groom. The groom was holding his arm, blood seeping through his fingers, and his own pistol was lying on the ground, where he'd obviously thrown it after he was shot.

'I am Mariah Fanshawe,' Jane said. 'What is the meaning of this outrage? How dare you attack my coach and wound my groom?'

Mariah had followed her from the carriage. She

was clearly a little dazed from the accident and still held the kerchief to her temple.

'She's the one we want.' One of the men holding a pistol trained on the coachman jerked his head at Jane. 'Let the other one get back inside.'

'I ain't sure she's the right one,' another of the rogues said. 'We'd best take them both to be certain. Blake will kick up if we get the wrong one.'

'We are not going anywhere,' Mariah put in, suddenly coming to life. 'Besides, I am Lady Fanshawe and my friend is lying to protect me. I demand that you allow us to continue our journey.'

'That settles it, we'll take them both,' the first rogue said and gestured at the groom and coachman. 'Get down and we'll take the carriage. Rab, you can drive. I'll get inside with the women.' He waved his pistol at them. 'Any funny business and I'll shoot yer.'

'Let Jane go on and I'll come with you,' Mariah offered.

'No, you can't,' Jane said and rushed to stand by her as the men hesitated, then one of them grabbed Mariah's arm and thrust her into the carriage. Jane saw the groom and coachman were obeying the men with the pistols and one of them had climbed up to the driving box as Mariah's servants got down. 'I shan't let you take her!' Jane flew at the man who was trying to push Mariah into the carriage and pulled the mask from his face. 'I've seen your face now. I shall know you again.'

'Take her, too.'

A new voice had spoken. Jane glanced over her shoulder and looked into the strangest pair of eyes she had ever seen. A scarf covered the bottom of the man's face, but his eyes were distinctive, being of odd colours.

'I'll know you, too,' she declared, her anger making her throw all caution to the winds. 'You had better let us…'

She got no further, for someone struck her on the back of the head and she made a little sighing noise as she fell into the arms of one of the men, who then thrust her into the carriage. She did not hear the gasp of distress from Mariah or see what happened next.…

* * *

Jane's eyelids flickered, but as the light touched her eyes she groaned. Becoming aware of pain at the back of her head, she reached towards the sore spot. She touched the bump gingerly and found a little crust of dried blood, though there was no deep wound. Something had hit her on the back of her head—but what?

Letting her eyes travel round the room, Jane knew that she had never seen it before in her life. This was not her room, but it did not look like an inn bedchamber. Her memory was fuzzy—where was she and how had she got here?

She closed her eyes for a moment as she puzzled over what had happened to her. Suddenly the details of the abduction flooded back.

Where was Mariah? Opening her eyes, Jane pushed herself up into a sitting position and looked about her. There was no sign of her friend and a shiver of dread ran through her.

She had evidently not been left in the same room as Jane. Was she somewhere in the house? Why had those villains been abducting her? It must surely be for her fortune. The rogues could not know that it was tied up in a fund and could only be released by her trustees. If they were expecting to be paid a ransom, they might be disappointed and what would happen then?

Jane was afraid for her friend. The kind of men who would hold up a coach, wound the groom and snatch two innocent women might be capable of anything. If their demands were refused, they might be violent towards their captives. Both she and Mariah might be in danger of their lives.

Glancing towards the window, she considered taking a look out when she heard voices outside the door of her room. Closing her eyes, she forced herself to lie still as the door was unlocked and someone came in. She made a little moaning sound as she sensed a presence near her and hoped that her captors would believe she was still unconscious.

'Damn that man Blake,' a man's voice said close to her. The voice was harsh, rough in tone. 'She is still unconscious. He must have hit her too hard. He is a thoughtless devil, for she may die—and then we'll be hung for sure if they catch us.'

'We should fetch a doctor,' another voice added.

This was a cultured voice, a gentleman's voice, but not one she knew. 'If she is ill, she may well die without attention. When I agreed to this business, I was told the other young woman was a willing participant in the plan. This girl should never have been abducted. What made him do it?'

'Blake couldn't afford to leave her behind. She might tell someone what she had seen—and he needs time with the other one.'

'Where has he taken her?' the second voice commanded.

'No idea. Captain Blake is a close-mouthed devil. Never lets his right hand know what his left hand is doing.'

'He is certainly a vicious brute.'

'What are we supposed to do with this girl? Blake doesn't want her. It would have been better to leave her on the road. The coachman would have taken care of her. I don't want to hang for her murder.'

'I have no intention of being hung for this affair. Blake struck this young woman. Until then I had no certainty of what was going on. I was hopeful that the Fanshawe girl truly wished to elope.'

'That tale won't help you if the Runners catch us. You'll hang with the rest of us if this goes wrong. We dare not fetch a doctor. The girl will be all right here for the moment. Blake will decide what to do when he comes.'

The men were moving away, leaving the room. Jane heard the door close and the key turn in the lock. She opened her eyes and breathed a sigh of relief. They had gone. She was alone, but she didn't intend to wait around for Blake to decide what to do with her. Jane didn't like the sound of the man they called Blake at all. She thought he must be the man with the odd colour eyes, one brown and the other a greenish colour that some called hazel. She'd looked into them seconds before he'd struck her.

Cautiously leaving the bed, she walked softly to the window and glanced out. She was in what appeared to be a private house in the country. From what she could see the grounds looked a little neglected, as if there wasn't quite enough money to keep them immaculate.

Now she knew why she was here. She had seen too much. Given the chance, Jane could have described the height, build and hair colouring of the men—and in particular the one with the peculiar eyes. Blake was obviously the ringleader. He'd kidnapped Mariah for her money—but what would he do to her when he realised that she had no power to release her fortune into his hands?

Jane hoped Mariah would somehow be able to fend the rogue off until help could be got for her.

If only Andrew had been with them! She was sure her brother would have done something to prevent the men snatching them both.

She must concentrate her thoughts. Somehow she had to get away from here and get help for her friend. Mariah was brave and resourceful. Had she been carrying her pistol she might have shot one of them—as she had the man who had been about to murder their good friend Lucinda, Duchess of Avonlea, earlier that year. Jane was a little comforted by the knowledge that Mariah would not be made a nervous wreck by the ab-duction. No, wherever Mariah was being held, she would hold her nerve and do her best to outwit her captor. Yet she could not hold out for ever against ruthless men.

Somehow Jane must get a message to Andrew—or, if he were still away on that mysterious mission with the army, to the Duke of Avonlea. He would surely try to help them if only because of the help he had received when his beloved wife was being blackmailed. To do that Jane must first escape her own captors.

She had a clear view of the gardens from her window. She noticed with some satisfaction that there was a large tree quite near her window. As she took stock, Jane saw a man riding away from the house and wondered where he was going. She drew back from the window, but he did not look in her direction.

Perhaps this was her chance to escape. Jane was about to attempt to open the window when she heard something. Realising that someone was coming back to her room, she made a dash for the bed, but it was too late.

She stood staring at the man who had entered and felt a trickle of ice from the nape of her neck down to the small of her back. He was carrying a tray with food and wine, which he set down on a small table near the bed. Jane decided he was not an ill-looking man. His features were regular and he had what she might have thought, in other circumstances, an attractive mouth. His hair was a rich brown, his eyes almost black with a hint of silver in the pupils. She was wary, but somehow not frightened.

'I thought you were faking it earlier,' he said and a rueful smile lingered on his mouth. 'You needn't be afraid I shall give you away. Nor shall I harm you. I am very sorry for the way you have been treated.'

It was the man with the cultured voice. He was wearing clothes that were not suited to his station—part of a disguise, she imagined. Yet she was certain that he was a gentleman. She relaxed and moved closer to him.

'I heard you mention someone called Blake. Is he the man with the odd-coloured eyes?'

He frowned. 'For your own sake, do not let anyone else hear you say that. It would be best not to let the others know that you heard us talking.'

'Who are you?' Jane asked. 'Why were you abducting Mariah? Is she here, too?'

'No, she was taken elsewhere. Do not ask more for I could not tell you. It is a complicated story and not one I am proud of. The pity is that you became involved. You should have stayed in the carriage rather than risking yourself,' the man said. 'I deeply regret that you were taken, Miss—?'

Jane's thoughts moved swiftly. She thought he was telling the truth when he said Mariah was elsewhere. She must have been brought here because the abductors did not know what to do with her.

'It is Jane—Jane Blair.'

Jane gave no sign of her inner trepidation as she offered her mother's maiden name. For the moment she would keep her true identity a secret.

'Well, Jane, I am sorry for helping those rogues with what has turned out to be a bad business. I am not sure what I can do for the moment. There are three others in the house besides myself and all are armed—but nothing more will happen to you if I can help it. You have my word that

I shall protect you from Blake and his lackeys somehow.'

'You said it would be best to fetch the doctor,' Jane said. 'Your friend said Blake would decide what to do—why do you serve him if he is such a monster? You appear to be a gentleman. Are you in trouble that you would stoop to such a wicked act?'

'It isn't what you think.' A dark colour stained his neck. 'These men are not my friends. Nor am I involved in this wretched affair for money—but I shan't tell you why, so don't ask.'

'What is your name?'

He hesitated, then, 'I'm called George by my friends.'

Jane was sure he was hiding something from her, but she should have expected it. He was hardly likely to tell her his life history under the circumstances.

'Are you intending to let me go?'

'I wish I could. Perhaps later.' George, as he called himself, looked uncomfortable. 'Most of the men have started to drink. Eat something and I'll see what I can do once they are off guard. If I tried to take you out of here by force, you might be killed. I might manage two of them, but three is too many. This needs careful planning.'

Jane glanced at the food. She was hungry, but more than that she was thirsty. However, she had no intention of touching anything this man had given her. He might be trying to poison her.

'There's nothing wrong with it,' he said. He took a piece of the bread, spread it with butter and ate it, then drank some wine. 'You won't die from eating this, Jane Blair.'

'Thank you. I might eat some later.' She moved towards him, making an appeal to his sense of fair play. 'If this Mr Blake is what you seem to imply, he will kill me, won't he? Do you want to hang for murder as well as abduction?'

'I don't want you to die.' He couldn't meet her eye. 'If we're caught, we'll hang anyway. I was told the other girl was willing. It was supposed to be an elopement made to look like abduction be-cause the girl's guardian wouldn't let her marry—but she was certainly not willing. I wasn't sure what was going on until Blake told them to take you, too. Obviously, I've been tricked into this sorry business. I was a damned fool to go along with it, but there were too many of them for me to stop it happening.'

Jane seized her opportunity. 'If you help me, we might be able to find her—and I wouldn't tell anyone you helped abduct us. You could be a hero and no one need know the truth.'

'You talk too much, Miss Blair,' he said and turned towards the door. 'Eat your food. If anyone else comes, pretend you don't know anything. I'll help you if I can. You have my word.'

'The word of a kidnapper?'

'Be careful, Miss Blair. I may be your only chance.'

His look was angry as he went out.

Jane sat on the edge of the bed as he locked the door again. Her legs felt like jelly and she was in sudden need of something to eat. After a few minutes to catch her breath, she took a piece of bread and spread it with butter, swallowing a few mouthfuls before washing it down with wine. The wine was a dark red and tasted dry on her tongue. She would have preferred water, but there was none in the room.

At least the food took away the shaky feeling she'd had in her legs. She wondered if he had told her the truth about there being three other men in the house. He called himself George. It wasn't his real name, of course, but it was something to fix in her mind. She'd heard him speak to someone else he hadn't named, and their leader was Blake.

Jane cautiously tried the window. It opened easily and she wondered why it hadn't been locked. Did they imagine that she could not escape from here? Perhaps most young women would not dare, but Jane had climbed trees from early childhood. She glanced at the tree, which was sturdy and grew to the right side of the window. She could climb out onto the wide stone window ledge and edge her way along to the tree. It would be a risk because there was still a small gap between the ledge and the nearest branch, but she thought she could probably do it if she tried.

Seeing two men riding towards the house, Jane closed the window and drew back, keeping watch from behind the curtain. The men dismounted and walked towards the main door, disappearing inside. Her head was throbbing, but she forced herself to think slowly and not panic. She could not dwell on how far up she was or how much her head hurt. Unless she took her chance now, she might die.

One of the riders was probably Blake. Had he come to tell them what to do with her? No doubt he would want her silenced for good. There was no time to lose. She must take her chance for escape now—or the ruthless Blake would almost certainly murder her and dispose of her body. The other men were wary of him. George had promised to help her, but she could not rely on his word. None of them would risk their own lives for hers.

Opening the window, Jane cautiously climbed out on to the ledge. At least it was in reasonable repair and felt solid beneath her feet. Her back pressed against the glass, she edged her way along the stone sill and then realised that she was too far from the branch to reach out and grab it. The branch itself was thick and substantial enough to take her weight, but there was a gap of perhaps two feet beyond what she could reach.

Jane's heart was racing and her palms were damp. She knew that she would have to jump and grab at the branch. If she missed, she might fall to the ground and break her neck, but if she stayed here the infamous Blake would undoubtedly break it for her.

Taking a deep breath and looking at the branch rather than the ground, Jane jumped and grabbed. Her hands touched, but could not hold the branch she was aiming for and she felt herself slithering and falling—but she was falling into the tree. Sharp bits of twig scratched her cheek and her bare arms as she crashed downwards and then, suddenly, she stopped. Her skirt had caught on a broken branch, breaking her fall a short distance from the ground.

Jane caught hold of a stout branch and clung to it as she recovered her breath and tried to stop shaking. She had come close to death and the shock was making her feel sick and weak, but her head was telling her she couldn't stay where she was for long. After a few seconds, she was able to think clearly again. She tugged at her gown, which held stubbornly to the branch for a few seconds before ripping and setting her free. Steadying herself with deep breaths, she clambered down and then fell the last few feet to her knees.

Jane's hands were stinging and so were her arms and legs. She glanced down and saw blood on her leg where the silk had torn away. Her right palm was bleeding and her cheek was stinging like mad, but these were not the worst of her injuries. As she stood up the pain in her right ankle shot through her and she gasped. Had she broken it? She tried to put weight on her right foot and found she could stand, though the pain was too bad for her to do more than limp.

She had to walk or hop as far as the woods that bordered the gardens. If the men looked for her and saw her here, they would recapture her easily. There was no choice but to hide somewhere until her ankle became a little easier. Let it be a sprain and not broken!

It was all she could do not to cry out each time she put her right foot to the floor, but she gritted her teeth and did a sort of hobble skip. Every movement hurt and she was afraid that someone would look out and see her before she reached the safety of the wood.

Fortune was with her. Battered, bruised but triumphant, Jane reached the trees and disappeared into them. She tasted the salt of tears on her mouth, but they were tears of relief and she brushed them away. It was impossible to move quickly and she knew she wasn't safe yet. The men were sure to come here as soon as they discovered she was missing.

Jane had to keep moving, but the pain in her ankle was getting worse and she wasn't sure how much farther she could go. She had almost reached the limit of her endurance when she saw the hut just ahead of her and hobbled towards it. The door opened easily and she went inside. She could make out a pile of old sacks in the darkness and sank down onto them.

She couldn't go any farther until she had rested her ankle. All she could do now was pray that the men would not find her.

Jane couldn't be sure how much time had passed when she heard the sounds of shouting.

Her stomach clenched; the voices were very near and she knew the men must be searching the wood for her. For a moment panic swept through her. She ought to have kept on walking, got as far away as possible. Perhaps she might have found help, but her ankle was still throbbing.

When the door of the shed started to open, Jane's heart jerked with fright. If Blake had found her, he might kill her.

Her breath caught as she saw George enter. He pushed the door almost closed behind him, putting a finger to his lips.

'Keep quiet. There's nothing I can do for the moment, but I'll come back later and help you. Wait for me.'

Jane opened her mouth to protest, but at a warning frown from him said nothing. Her chest felt tight and she could scarcely breathe as he went out again.

'Anything in there?'

The voice was so close. Harsh and angry, she was sure it must be Blake and her heart hammered in her breast. If he came in and found her…but she could hear George answering him.

'Just some old sacks. I told you she would be long gone by now. Why would she hang around here?'

'The lot of you are damned fools. Why didn't you tie her up or at least make sure she was in a room she couldn't get out of?'

'She must have climbed into the tree,' a third voice said on a whining note. 'You've got to admire a girl like that, Captain. It took a lot of pluck. Besides, what harm can she do? She doesn't know who we are or what is going on.'

'She hadn't better or I shall know who to blame,' the harsh voice muttered. 'I suppose she's gone now and there's not much we can do about it. She saw my eyes, but if she doesn't know my name it is a chance in a million that she can identify me.'

'How could she know who you are?' George said. 'We should go back to the house. I have things to do. I only agreed to help with this because I thought the Fanshawe girl willing, Blake. Though it leaves a bad taste in my mouth, I've fulfilled my part of the deal. I want what you owe me and an end to this whole rotten business.'

'You'll get what I promised when I'm good and ready—which will be when I get what I want.'

'That isn't what we agreed…'

Jane heard the angry note in George's voice as the men moved away. He had told her his motive was not money, so what did Blake have that was so important to George that he would help abduct an innocent young woman to get his hands on it?

He had told her to trust him, but what kind of a man was he?

Shivering, Jane hugged herself and wondered if she should try to get away on her own once the men had gone. She wasn't sure she would be wise to trust George—yet he had discovered her hiding place and kept it secret.

Jane walked to the door of the shed and stopped. If anything, her ankle felt worse than just after she had sprained it. It seemed as if she didn't really have a choice. She would just have to wait and hope that George kept his word.

Night had fallen and Jane was beginning to turn cold when she heard something outside the hut. Then the door opened and a dark shadow entered. Her heart caught as she held her breath and waited for him to speak.

'Are you there, Jane Blair?'

'George?' Her breath expelled in relief as she hobbled towards him. 'I was beginning to think you had forgotten me.'

'It took a while to get rid of the others and circle back,' George said. 'I didn't want to arouse their suspicions. Blake is a nasty devil when his temper is up. I shouldn't be surprised if what they say of him is true.'

'What do they say?'

'That he…well, he is supposed to have been thrown out of the army for causing the death of ten French prisoners during the campaign on the Spanish Peninsula in a particularly nasty manner. He is a bully and a cheat, I know that much, but I've never been certain of the rest.'

'What does he owe you? What hold has he over you?'

Jane looked up at him. They had moved outside the hut and the moon had just sailed out from behind the clouds. For a moment she glimpsed an odd expression in his eyes, but in another moment it had gone.

'It isn't my secret. I can't tell you,' he said. 'I know it must be hard for you to trust me after what has happened, but, believe me, this is the first thing I've ever done that I feel truly ashamed of—and I had a compelling reason. I just cannot tell you what it is.'

Jane gazed at him for a little longer, then inclined her head. 'Perhaps I am foolish, but I do trust you, George. I trust you—and I am grateful for your help. I hurt my ankle when I fell through the tree and I can hardly walk.'

'I knew it must be something of the sort when I found you here.' A smile flickered at the corners of his mouth. 'You must have jumped from the ledge to the tree. It takes courage to do something like that.'

'My brother would say it was reckless and foolish—but I thought my life might be in danger.'

'It might have been, had Blake found you himself. He was furious that we let you escape. For a few minutes I thought he would shoot us all, but it seems he may still have a use for us.'

'Would you go to the law if you were not in such an awkward position?'

'I could be hung for my part in the affair,' George said. 'Yet if I could be sure… What happened has left a sour taste in my mouth. I wish with all my heart I could go back to the start, but it is too late for regret. I am in this up to my neck. The only thing I can do is to help you get away.'

'I cannot walk far.'

'Lean on me—or shall I carry you? My horse is not far away. It will support us both until we can find somewhere to stop and rest while I take a look at your ankle.'

'If you could find a horse I could borrow, I could go home. I have no money with me, but I will repay whatever you spend on my behalf.'

'The hire of a horse would be little enough,' George said. 'I'm not sure it will be safe for you to go home just yet, Miss Blair—especially alone. Blake means to search for you.'

'He cannot know who I am or where I live?'

'I dare say your family will be looking for you—making enquiries, perhaps even offering a reward.' George heard her indrawn breath and nodded. 'It will not take Blake long to discover who you really are—and if you are sitting at home he may take things into his own hands. Once he has what he wants and takes himself off abroad, you should be safe enough, but until then...'

'Until then my life is at risk? And my friend's?'

'I fear it may be so.'

'What shall I do?'

'I'm not sure. I've been thinking what to do for the best. It may be expedient to stay hidden for a while.'

'What about you? Are you afraid that I shall betray you to the authorities?'

Jane winced as she took a step forwards. George hesitated, then swept her up in his arms, carrying her to where his horse was tethered. He thrust her up into the saddle, then mounted behind her.

'Press back against me and hang on to the saddle. I'm going to ride hard for a bit. Blake might get suspicious and come looking for us. If he finds us, it will not be just you he murders.'

Jane was silent as she obeyed, holding on tight

as he put his horse to a canter, then urged the animal on faster as it gathered speed. George had not answered her question.

It was obviously her duty to tell someone all she knew as swiftly as she was able. Mariah was in terrible danger, because Jane was certain that Blake was a ruthless man. If he discovered that Mariah's fortune was tied up in trust and could not be released, he might decide it was best to kill her.

She had to escape and get help for Mariah! Now that she was with George her own fears had become less acute and it was her friend's safety that worried her.

Riding through the darkness, her body pressed close to that of the man who had rescued her and now held her in his arms, Jane thought hard.

Could she escape George—or would it be best to befriend him and ask for his help in tracing Mariah?

'Thank God you are back!' Justin, Duke of Avonlea, exclaimed as he was admitted to Andrew Lanchester's parlour and found him still dressed in his travelling cape, his boots spattered with mud. 'I thought you might still be in Paris.'

'I have just this moment arrived,' Andrew said and frowned. 'Something is wrong—Lucinda has not disappeared again?'

'My wife is at home and in good health,' Avonlea said, a smile on his lips. Then the smile disappeared as he recalled his news. 'I am very sorry, Lanchester, but the news I bring must distress you. Your sister and Mariah Fanshawe were abducted this morning on the road to London...'

'Mariah—Jane! Good grief.' Andrew looked thunderstruck. 'Why? Where were they going?'

'Mariah received an invitation from Sir Matthew Horne and his wife—she is the late Fanshawe's sister, of course. Mariah did not wish to go for some reason and would only consent to it if Jane accompanied her. The two have become such good friends of late.'

'Damn!' Andrew smote his forehead with his fist. 'Did Mariah not tell you she was afraid of fortune hunters when she came to stay with you some months back, Avonlea?'

'You think she may have been abducted by a scorned suitor?'

'That is possible,' Andrew replied and looked thoughtful. 'Mariah is something of a flirt, I imagine. She might have led someone to believe she was interested and then changed her mind.'

'Desperate men will do anything for money.' Avonlea looked at him enquiringly. 'Why should they take Jane, too?'

'If they were together and the abductor believed Mariah to be travelling alone he might have acted on impulse. Jane can be very rash at times. She might have tried to obstruct them.'

'You think she may have been taken because of what she saw?'

'I fear that may be the case. She would not let her friend be taken without putting up a fight.'

'Brave but foolish.'

'I have told her to be careful a hundred times, but she puts her heart over her fences. Jane ought truly to have been my brother rather than my sister—and in part that is my fault. After our parents' death I treated Jane as an equal. We were inseparable until I joined up, and since then she has looked after the estate for me. I fear she is too independent and perhaps reckless—but I would trust her judgement above any agent.'

'You have only just arrived, so you will not know if a ransom note has been received,' Avonlea said. 'Mariah's coachman came to me at once, but nothing has been delivered to me. Of course, the note might be addressed to the trust-ees of her fortune.'

'You are not her trustee?'

'No. I believe they are Fanshawe's sister—and a lawyer. No doubt they will be approached for the ransom if a demand is made.'

'It must have been Mariah they were after. I know nothing of her fortune, but I imagine Fanshawe was a warm man. Jane has only a few thousand. I would pay for her return, of course—but I doubt she was the intended victim.'

'What will you do?'

'I must visit Mariah's trustees and discover if they have been approached—and I shall instruct an agent to discover what they can. What will you do?'

'A Bow Street man? Good idea,' Avonlea agreed.

'In your situation I think it the best solution. I think you should leave Mariah's trustees to me, Andrew. Instruct your agent by all means. I will talk to Sir Matthew and see what I can discover— then I'll report to you.'

'Yes, I dare say you are anxious for Mariah's sake. She is like a sister to you, I believe?'

'She was my father's ward until he died, and of course Lucinda has become very fond of her,' Justin said. 'I know Mariah intended to ask my advice about some fortune hunter, but perhaps because of various problems it never happened. I feel responsible and must certainly do what I can to help recover her.'

'Then we shall work together.'

'Of course. You know I was grateful for your help with my problems.' Avonlea smiled. 'We may not always have seen eye to eye over the methods you employed, Andrew—but we are friends, and in this we are united.'

'Yes. Good grief, I need all the help I can get,' Andrew said and frowned. 'I suppose the ladies' abduction is for a ransom? Only I've been involved in a bit of business—secret stuff for the regiment that I cannot reveal even to you—but it might have a bearing.'

'Well, you know your own business best—but I shall do what I can to recover them both.'

'I pray to God that they are both still alive.'

'Yes.' Justin looked grim. 'I can imagine how you feel. I suffered enough when my wife disappeared—but she was found unharmed and I believe we shall come through this in good order, Andrew.'

'I can only pray that your instincts are correct.'

Chapter Two

They seemed to have been riding for hours. Jane was beginning to think she was in some kind of mad dream that would never end when George at last brought his horse to a standstill and helped her to dismount.

'Where are we?' she asked, glancing towards the house, which looked silent and dark in the gloom of night. 'Who lives here?'

'No one at present,' George replied. 'It belonged to a relative of mine and has recently been left to me in a will. I have been meaning to visit and have it set in order.'

'Are there any servants?' she enquired in a dubious tone that made her companion look at her.

'No, I fear not,' George answered. 'I know

it is asking a great deal—but you have to trust me, Jane.'

'You do realise that if I stay in an empty house with you for even an hour or so my reputation could be ruined?'

'Yes, I know that it is a risk, but I really think we both need some rest. I have food. I dare say I can get a fire going and we shall find somewhere to curl up and sleep. I promise you are quite safe with me, Miss Blair—and no one need know the details. In the morning I shall take you some-where more suitable—at least, to a place where you can be chaperoned.'

'I really have no choice,' Jane admitted rue-fully. When she reflected on her capture, she re-alised that she had been compromised from the beginning. While most would sympathise, oth-ers would think her at fault for her reckless be-haviour. 'My ankle is throbbing and I shall fall asleep in the saddle if we go any farther tonight.'

'Exactly.' George smiled at her in a way that calmed her fears. 'Truly, I mean you no harm, Miss Blair—and I shall endeavour to get us both out of this mess.'

'I prefer it when you call me Jane,' she said. 'Our situation makes formality ridiculous. I have no choice but to call you by your name or sir. In the circumstances I think we should forget convention. Since we are forced into each other's company, I suppose we must make the best of things.'

'How sensible you are. I have seldom met a lady with your strength of character, Jane. Most of the ladies I know would have screamed or fainted given the situation you found yourself in.'

'You need not tell me that I am too independent for modesty's sake. It has been said before and not so politely.' Jane laughed softly. 'Had I been so faint-hearted I might never have been abducted. I dare say my brother will scold me for being reckless and thoughtless—and I believe I may owe you my life. The loss of my reputation can be nothing compared to what might have been.'

He inclined his head to her, applauding her courage. 'Just so—now we should turn our minds to gaining entrance. I think I may have to break a window and climb through. You must wait here.

I shall open a door and save you the indignity of clambering over the sill.'

Jane studied the small leaded windows. 'Are there no French windows? I fear these windows would scarcely open wide enough for a man of your size.'

'Yes, there is such a window at the rear. That is an excellent notion, Jane. Much better than a window, through which I might find it difficult to fit.'

'I do not think you would make a competent burglar,' Jane said, her humour asserting itself as she followed him to the rear of the house. There was no use in repining or complaining. They found the glass doors, which led out to the pretty and secluded garden. George stood looking at it for a moment, seemingly in deep thought. 'What will you use to break the window? Or had you not thought so far?'

'There you wrong me. I was merely remembering some good times I had here as a boy. It seems sacrilege to disturb the place, but it must be done.' George took a pistol from his coat pocket, and turning the handle against the glass, gave it a sharp rap. It shattered at once. He pushed the jagged glass in and put his hand through the opening. Finding the catch which secured it, he was able to open the door.

'I shall go first and light a candle,' George said. 'Be careful for there is broken glass. I do not wish you to stumble in the dark and hurt yourself.'

Jane hesitated just inside the door, allowing him time to explore. A few seconds passed and she heard him strike a tinder and then light flared in the darkness. He lit a branch of wax candles, the yellow glow illuminating the pretty if neglected parlour in which she now stood. She looked about her with interest, noting the delicate furniture, workbasket, spinet and the French cabinets filled with porcelain figurines.

'This parlour must have belonged to a lady.'

'Yes, it did—an elderly lady. She was my great-aunt and more than ninety years of age when she died.'

'I hope she would not mind us breaking in?'

'I should imagine she might find it exciting. I believe she was rather a dashing lady in her youth. She took a shine to me because I was con-

sidered a bruising rider to hounds as a young-
ster—and she was fond of hunting herself.'

'A lady after my own heart, though it is the
thrill of the chase I love. I usually leave the field
before the kill.'

'Aunt Augusta would not have approved of
that,' he said and smiled. 'However, I seldom hunt
these days. I saw enough death and killing in the
army. I have no desire for more.'

'Yet you joined forces with a dangerous man to
help abduct an innocent young woman.' Her tone
was accusing and made him look at her.

'I have no excuse I may give other than that I
have already offered. I believed I was helping to
provide the illusion of an abduction. Until she
struggled so desperately I hoped the lady was
willing, as I had been led to believe.'

'Yes, so you told me.' Jane frowned as he led
the way from the small parlour into another larger
one, then into a hall, through several more reception rooms and finally a large kitchen at the rear.
It was still painful for her to walk, though a little
easier than it had been when he found her in the

hut. 'I find it hard to believe that you were duped, sir. I would not take you for a fool.'

'I had my reasons.'

Jane glanced at the grim set of his mouth and said no more on the subject. It would not do to antagonise him at this point. She must never forget that Mariah was in danger and this man was perhaps her only chance of finding her friend.

'I think the fireplace in the larger parlour was set with wood and paper,' she said. 'It would be more relaxing than the kitchen for there are some comfortable chairs.'

'I thought we might find some wine here…' George disappeared into what looked like a storeroom. Jane heard him rummaging around for a moment or two. He emerged triumphant with a bottle of red wine. 'There are several bottles here, though most must be in the cellar, but I have no intention of going there at this hour.'

Jane found another branch of candles and lit them from his. Her ankle was throbbing and she sat down at the table, trying not to show how weary she felt.

'Shall we explore further or settle on the parlour?'

'I think the beds must need airing. It is more than a year since the house was closed. My lawyers thought it best while I was in the army. I believe a caretaker comes in now and then, but I doubt the bedding is fit to use.'

'We shall do better in a comfortable chair,' Jane said. 'If you are agreeable, I shall light the fire in the parlour.'

'I shall do that for you. We should eat and then I will look at your ankle. I think cold water and a bandage—which should be in the dresser if all is as it was.' He went to the dresser and took out a tin, opening it to extract a roll of linen. 'My aunt was always prepared. I think I must fetch water from the well.'

'I will wait for you in the parlour.'

'Forgive me, your ankle still pains you. Go and sit down. I will bring food and the bandage in a moment or two.'

Jane took the candles she had lit and retraced her steps to the large parlour. She lit several more and then touched a flame to the fire. It flared almost at once, which meant the wood and paper had kept dry despite the house being closed for so long. The house was clearly not damp and must be well built.

Her situation was improved despite the impropriety of it all. George seemed to mean her no harm and for the moment she must trust him, though it irked her to be at the mercy of a rogue. She was used to being independent and using her own judgement, and this need of a stranger's help was both uncomfortable and annoying.

Seeing the elegant day bed, Jane settled back on the cushions and rested her foot in front of her. With the candles and the fire, which was now burning strongly, it was pleasant and comfortable. She put her head back and closed her eyes, quickly falling asleep.

Returning to the parlour some minutes later, George stood looking at Jane, feeling disinclined to disturb her. Yet the bread and cheese he had brought with him was on the plates he had found in the kitchen, the wine poured into glasses—and her ankle would do better if he bound it.

'Forgive me, Miss…Jane,' he said and touched her shoulder.

Jane woke with a little start, giving a cry of alarm. Then, seeing him standing there, a tray of food placed carefully on the occasional table by her side, and the linen bandaging in his hand, she smiled. The smile came from within and lit up her eyes. She had such calm grey eyes and her dark, almost ebony hair had fallen into tangles where it had escaped from the knot at the nape of her neck. She was not beautiful in a conventional sense, but had a face filled with character and warmth.

'It is you,' she said. 'For a moment I thought… How thoughtless of me to fall asleep. You must be wanting your supper.'

George's heart caught when she smiled. She was an attractive girl, but he had not thought her more until that moment. He wondered that she wore such dull colours and scraped her hair back in an unflattering style when she could make so much more of herself if she chose.

'I was thinking of you, Jane. Your ankle needs

a cold compress and ought to be bound tightly to take down the swelling.'

'Yes, I am sure that would help. I feared it might be broken, but the pain has eased a little, which means, I think, that it is merely a sprain.'

He knelt on the floor beside her and ran gentle, sensitive fingers over her ankle, then inclined his head.

'I believe it is as you say, Jane. Nevertheless, it will help to have a cold compress and bandaging for a while. We shall not stay here long tomorrow, so it will be better for you if your ankle is easier.'

George worked steadily, applying the cold pack he had prepared with water drawn from the deep well. He bound her ankle tightly, knowing that it would strengthen it for her, making it easier to walk. She drew a sharp breath once and he apologised for hurting her, but she shook her head. He finished his work as quickly as possible.

'If you are still in pain, I will bind the ankle again in the morning,' he said. 'Can you eat something? The wine is soft and fruity, not too strong—will you try a little before I leave you to sleep?'

'Where will you go? The room is warm now and you could stretch out in two chairs.'

'Are you sure you wish for that? I thought you might prefer to be alone?'

'We broke in here and the door is vulnerable. If Blake were to discover this house I would rather not face him alone.'

'I doubt he would think of coming here.' George frowned. 'Though it is possible that he might know it was left to me, I suppose. Someone may have told him.'

'Then please remain here. I prefer your presence to Captain Blake's.'

'Yes, I think I shall. You may rest assured that if he attacked you I should shoot him.'

'Is that why you have brought the pistol?'

'Like most military men I am accustomed to travelling with a loaded pistol. I know others do it, too, but I am a keen shot. Believe me—my hand would not tremble if the need arose.'

'You fought with Wellington?'

'Yes, for many years—on the Spanish Peninsula and elsewhere.'

'I see.' Jane looked at him thoughtfully. 'I

believe I shall sleep more easily for knowing that, sir.'

'You have my word that I shall protect you with my life. More than that I cannot promise. Blake is a ruthless devil and has several rogues working for him that think nothing of murder. Had I not known that he might kill us all, I should have prevented the abduction as soon as I realised that he had lied about the lady's willingness to be taken.'

'Even though he has something important that belongs to you?'

'Yes, of course.' George inclined his head. 'Had it been within my power. As it was not, I decided to do what I could for you.'

'What of the other victim in this affair? Lady Fanshawe is a dear friend of mine and I fear for her safety. Can you not help her?'

'For the moment I can do nothing, but I shall try to discover her whereabouts. For that reason I have allowed Blake to go on thinking he has my reluctant loyalty.'

'Every moment we delay, her situation becomes more desperate.'

'You should not fear that her life is in immediate danger. Blake wants her alive until he has her fortune safe in his hands. If she died before he persuades her to wed him, he would lose what he truly wants—though he swears he cares for her and she for him. Were I not sure that he means her no harm for the moment, I should have gone to the authorities immediately. I am in part to blame for her predicament and shall do what I can to help her.'

'Do you believe Blake when he says he cares for her?'

'Not any longer. Yet I think she is safe enough for the time being—at least, her life is not at risk. More than that is not within my power to judge.'

'He may allow her to live, but she may lose everything else,' Jane reminded him. 'Abduction and the forceful seduction of an innocent lady is a wicked crime. Rogues who participate in such crimes deserve to hang.'

A little nerve flicked at George's temple. Yet his expression was strictly controlled, giving no hint of his state of mind.

'I cannot deny it. Nor do I deny that I played a part in this heinous affair. I wish it were otherwise—though had I not agreed to help him, he would have employed some other rogue. I should not then have been in a position to help you—or her.'

Jane silently acknowledged the truth of his words as she ate her food and swallowed a few mouthfuls of wine. She undoubtedly owed the fact that she was still alive to him, for had he not found her in the hut and then denied it to his companions, Blake might have come himself. She might already be lying dead somewhere. Putting the wineglass down still half-full, she sighed and leaned back to rest her head on the comfortable cushions. She was inclined to believe George when he said he regretted taking part in the abduction of Mariah Fanshawe, but that did not excuse his conduct. Whatever the hold Blake had over him, he should not have sunk to that vile creature's level.

Within a few minutes of finishing her wine, Jane had once again fallen asleep. Watching her, George felt oddly protective. He bent to place another log on the fire. It was most unlikely that

Blake would come here, but he would wedge something heavy against the French windows they had broken to enter. He would try not to sleep, though he knew he was tired and might not be able to keep guard throughout the night despite his best intentions.

George was thoughtful as he went off to make sure that the house was as secure as he could make it. Jane Blair—if that was her true name—was a remarkable young woman. He thought that if he had met her in other circumstances he might not have noticed her, for he was more usually attracted to ladies with pale hair and blue eyes. There had once been a lady with beautiful azure eyes who had stolen, then broken his heart. It was because of Marianne that he had run off and joined the army, wanting release from the pain she had caused. However, he had quickly forgotten her in the heat of battle, the sight of fallen comrades driving what he now realised was a mere fancy from his mind.

George was not now the same feckless daredevil he had been in his youth. Had Marianne accepted his proposal he would probably have broken her heart a dozen times. He had not been ready for marriage and Marianne in her wisdom had known it. Now, having seen too much fighting and too much pain, he had returned to England to settle down, perhaps here at the estate that his great-aunt had left him. His own father had had no other son and George had inherited the greater part of his estate, which was not large, and part of which had gone to the sister he adored. He was not the richest man in England, but his great-aunt's estate had given him the money he needed to retire from the army and build a new life in England. Having a true interest in wine, he was contemplating setting up a business to import fine vintages from Spain and Portugal.

Thinking of his sister, George's brow furrowed. It was because of Verity that he was in this predicament, hiding from a man George despised and disliked. Blake had some letters and personal effects that belonged to Verity and she had begged George to recover them for her.

Blake was still withholding Verity's property, refusing to give George what he had promised. He was not sure what he could do about his sister's problem. Unless he took desperate measures and broke into the rogue's house.

It was perhaps what he should have done at the beginning, George acknowledged to himself. The one thing he ought not to have done was to let Blake blackmail him into helping with his evil plans. He was not even sure why Blake had wanted him involved—unless he'd thought to gain a hold over George, too, which in part he had for he was now guilty of a heinous crime. Yet had he not agreed, Jane might even now be dead—and the abduction would have gone ahead anyway. At least now there was a chance that he could help one, or perhaps both, of the ladies.

He was determined that nothing should happen to Jane Blair. Her bravery in escaping and the way she faced having to stay with a man she did not know in an empty house made him admire her. Verity would have been in hysterics by now. Jane was an exceptional young woman and he would protect her with his life.

Jane was woken by the smell of coffee and bacon frying. She blinked hard, easing her stiff shoulders as she looked for the source of the delicious aroma. Seeing the tray of hot food on the table beside her, she glanced up at the man who had provided the feast.

'How did you find these?' she asked as he poured the steaming liquid into two delicate porcelain cups. 'Bacon, eggs, fresh bread—and coffee?'

'The caretaker, Mrs Muffet, saw candles here last evening. She came to investigate at first light. I explained that I had come down from London to look at the house and she insisted on fetching food from her cottage and cooking it for us.'

'You told her I was here? What does she know?'

'I told her I had a friend with me. She did not come in here and does not know that my friend is a lady. I allowed her to think you were a gentleman.'

'Thank you.' Jane accepted the coffee from his hand. 'It was very good of Mrs Muffet to provide these things for us.'

'She intends to return later today and make the house habitable. I have asked that fires should be lit in all the rooms and the linen aired.'

'You are not intending to stay here? Impossible!' Jane took a sip of the hot strong beverage to calm her nerves. 'At least, I cannot stay here. Perhaps you would lend me your horse and allow me to go on alone? I will engage to return it here once I am home.'

'I dare not let you leave alone. You would be prey to all manner of evils, a young woman travelling alone with not even a groom to protect her.'

'I believe I am capable of riding a few miles to my home—if you would set me in the right direction.' Jane's head came up for she needed no one to protect her. 'I am not one of your missish young ladies who faints at the merest provocation.'

'I am perfectly certain you are not, Jane. I wish that I could deliver you to your home,' George said, his brow furrowed. 'I have been thinking and I believe I have come up with a solution, which you may find acceptable for a few days.'

Jane arched her brows at him. 'Short of stealing your horse and riding off, I have little choice but to listen to your proposal, sir. My ankle is a little easier this morning, but I do not think I could walk far—and I have no money to hire a carriage.'

'I am aware of my duty to care for you. Will you allow me to take you to the home of a lady I trust? She was my nurse when I was a boy and stayed with us until she retired when I joined the army. I think you should be safe with her until I can be certain Blake is out of the country—or in prison.'

'In prison? Do you intend to go to the magistrate, then?'

George handed her a plate of crisp bacon and scrambled eggs, also a two-pronged fork. 'You should eat some of this excellent food. Please, do not look at me so, Miss Blair. I know that I deserve your censure, but you do not understand my predicament.'

'I realise that Captain Blake has some hold over you, but that does not excuse your behaviour. No decent man would assist in the abduction of an innocent young woman.' Seeing the little nerve flicking at his temple, Jane relented. 'Forgive me, I am not ungrateful for all you have done for me, sir. It is just that I am concerned for my friend.'

'As I am,' George replied. 'You have no need to remind me of my responsibility. Firstly, I must see you safe, Miss Blair—and then I shall do what I can to find Lady Fanshawe.'

Jane was on thorns. Her independent nature made her wish to escape by whatever means she could. Yet she sensed that George meant to do what he could to help her—and if she ran away now she would have no clue to give her friends. If she could just discover something about Captain Blake, her friends might be able to find and rescue Mariah.

'You give me your word that you will try to find her? And you will see that Blake pays for his wickedness?'

'I promise that I shall do what I can, but I am not at liberty to go to the magistrates immediately.'

George reached across the table, laying his hand on hers. It was a simple gesture, but something in his manner made her decide that he was honest and meant to do what he could for both her and Mariah.

'Then I shall seriously consider what you've said, sir.'

'Good.' His smile lit up his face and for a moment Jane's heart caught. 'You are a brave and sensible lady, Jane.'

Jane ate some of the bacon and egg, then finished her coffee. Her thoughts were confused, but she was trying to make sense of what she knew to be a precarious situation. If Captain Blake was as ruthless as she believed, she could hardly demand that this man risk his own life more than he already had for her sake.

'I know that you have risked your life for mine, sir—and I believe you are doing what you think best, but I am anxious for Mariah.'

'I understand your anxiety, but first I must make certain that you are safe—after that I shall do what I can to help your friend.'

'I have no wish to be that evil rogue's next victim,' Jane replied. 'However, I am concerned that Blake will harm Mariah. If that happened, I should not be able to live with my conscience—as you ought not.'

'You must trust me,' George said. 'Your friend

may be confined anywhere. Even if we managed to have Blake arrested and called out the militia to search for her, we might not find her. If she is bound or securely confined in a secluded house, she might die alone and in terrible distress. On the other hand, Blake's interest is in keeping her alive and well until she consents to wed him.'

Jane looked at him in horror. 'You think Blake would refuse to reveal her whereabouts if he were arrested?'

'Why should he confess when it would hang him? At the moment it is my word against his. Even with you as a witness it is not certain that we should be believed—and I should be reluctant to involve you for it would inevitably result in a loss of reputation for you. If Blake were to remain at liberty, my life would be at risk.'

'And mine. I saw his eyes and he knows it.'

'Exactly. Which is another reason why it is best if you remain hidden. Your testimony may be required to convict him since mine may not be believed, though I shall keep you out of it if I can. However, he has only to murder us both and there would be none left who dare speak against him.'

'Yes, I see that,' Jane agreed reluctantly. 'So what must we do?'

'If you will consent to remain hidden, I shall do my utmost to discover Lady Fanshawe's whereabouts and to rescue her.'

'Do you give me your word?'

'You have my word, but I must be allowed to do things my way. Lady Fanshawe's life is not the only one at risk here. If she is forced into marriage against her will, an annulment might be arranged.'

'She would be ruined in the eyes of society.'

'Lady Fanshawe is a victim and most will have sympathy for her. Another person's happiness is at stake here and I have a duty to that person. I see you condemn me—but I am caught between duty and loyalty.'

Jane saw that he was deeply affected. It was a terrible coil and she found herself unable to condemn him as certainly as she had. He had become embroiled in an unpleasant affair for reasons he was not prepared to divulge. While she condemned the wicked abduction of an innocent young woman, she had begun to realise that George's motives were compelling. He had acted out of a misguided attempt to help someone he was protecting.

'So Blake is blackmailing you?'

'Not me—but there is blackmail involved.'

'Yes, I understand.' Jane nodded. 'I see how you were tricked into helping that rogue, but now you must do all you can to make this right. I will stay with your nurse for a day or so, but it cannot be longer. My brother will be anxious.'

'Perhaps I could send a letter for you—if you will give me your name? Your true name, for I do not believe you are called Jane Blair.'

'I shall think about it,' Jane replied. 'If you will allow me some privacy, I shall make myself ready and then perhaps we should leave. For the moment I am content to do as you ask.'

'Thank you.' George hesitated, then leaned forwards to kiss her cheek. Jane moved her head inadvertently and his mouth brushed hers in the lightest of kisses. 'Thank you for believing in me, Jane. I've never met such a brave and decisive lady before. Most ladies of my acquaintance would have been in floods of tears long before this.'

Jane blushed, her heart racing. How ridiculous! He'd meant only to kiss her cheek as a thank-you, but the feel of his lips on hers had sent a tingle racing through her, which was ridiculous because she had long ago given up all thought of love and marriage.

She was not the sort of woman men admired or wanted as their wives; her independence and habit of speaking her mind actually repulsed men who might otherwise have thought her a suitable match. Although not without fortune, she was plain and too outspoken to please generally.

'Nonsense,' she said and turned away, a flush in her cheeks. 'Crying would change nothing. We must think of Mariah and do what is best for her.'

'You have discovered a clue?' Justin asked. He glanced at Andrew. 'Pray do not keep me in suspense. Does this concern Mariah or your sister?'

'I made some enquiries myself and discovered that the carriage used for the abduction of Mariah and Jane turned off before reaching the toll. I therefore rode across country and was able to discover that a few miles from Avonlea an unconscious lady was seen being transferred from one carriage to another. I have been told that both carriages then set off in different directions.'

'I am not sure what this means.'

'We believe that Mariah was indeed the intended victim.' Justin nodded. 'It seems to me that Mariah was taken off by one of them and several men remained with the first carriage in which Jane was taken somewhere else.'

'Yes, that would appear to be the logical explanation. So your search has been split—a clever ruse to confuse the situation, perhaps?'

'After employing the agent I told you of, I made a further search myself and was able to trace Mariah's carriage to its final destination. Indeed, I discovered it still at the property, where it had been abandoned.'

'You have discovered one of the ladies?'

'Unfortunately not,' Andrew replied. 'The house was deserted, but there were signs of it having been used recently. By the look of it no one had been there for years until one of the captives was taken there. It was because it had fallen into disuse that I was guided there by a curious bystander. He had worked up at the hall, as he called it, and knew that the old man had died. The owner had no immediate family and died intestate, which meant the land and property had been neglected while lawyers attempted to find the rightful beneficiaries.'

'It will, of course, go to the Crown if none are found, but left to decay it will fetch little enough. What made your informant so curious?'

'The carriage swept past him and frightened a flock of sheep he was driving into new pasture. One of them injured itself and he was angry so he went up to the house to remonstrate and saw a woman being carried into the house. He thought she was unconscious, but, apart from telling his wife, he did nothing more until he heard that I was making enquiries at the local inn. I paid him a guinea, which was recompense for the animal's injuries and he described the carriage and one of the men he saw.'

'But when you went to the house it was empty?'

'I found a back door open and went in. I

searched every room. One bedroom had been oc-
cupied. The bed looked as if someone had lain on
it and there was a tray of food and wine. The window was unlatched. There were signs of people
having been elsewhere in the house—but nothing
to tell me who might have been there.' Andrew
paused and his mouth thinned. 'However, in the
bedroom, I found a reticule that belongs to my
sister. She must have had it with her when they
took her to the house and left it there on the floor
by the bed.'

'Then you can be certain she was in the house,'
Avonlea said. 'Did you find blood or the signs
of a struggle?'

'No, thank God!' Andrew rubbed at the side
of his nose. 'I saw some branches that had broken recently in a tree near the open window. I
believe—I have hope that—Jane may have got
out of that window and scrambled down through
the tree.'

Justin stared at him in disbelief. 'Is it possible?
Would she have tried to escape that way?'

'Yes, I am sure she would if she had the chance.'

Andrew frowned. 'I spent some time looking in the wood near the house. I found some deep tracks—as if a horse might be carrying two people.'

'Did they recapture her?'

'That, too, is possible. I know that Jane would do her best to get word to me if she could.'

'Were you not engaged on some business or other for the regiment?'

'That business is on hold,' Andrew said. 'If Jane and Mariah are not found, I must leave the matter to another, because I shall not rest until I know they are safe. Just as you cannot rest until Mariah is found.'

Avonlea nodded. 'My wife is concerned for Mariah, as I am. You have not received a ransom note?'

'No. I am certain the rogue means to compromise Mariah, perhaps even force her into marriage for the sake of her fortune.'

'Yet her trustees have heard nothing. I told them what had happened and they were greatly distressed. They begged me to find Mariah and see her safely wed to a decent man—and I have promised to do all I can, but Mariah has a mind of her own. Apparently, they have the power to veto a marriage if they think it unsuitable, but I was assured that if I approved the match they would not object.'

'You do not think she agreed to this abduction to force her trustees to release her money?'

'Mariah is inclined to be reckless, but she would not endanger a friend. Had this been a sham abduction, Mariah would simply have disappeared and a note been immediately delivered. I think the rogue that has taken her means to hold out for marriage to ensure he has the whole of her fortune.'

'What will her trustees do if he makes such a demand?'

'I have been asked to manage the affair to prevent a scandal. If she is forced into anything, her abductor will very soon regret it.'

'Be careful, Justin,' Andrew said. 'Whoever planned this is a clever devil. He will not simply hand Mariah over. You may have to release at least a part of her fortune if you wish to see her safe.'

'Damn it, I don't care for the money—but the rogue deserves to hang.'

'Yes, he does,' Andrew agreed. 'If I have anything to say in the matter, that is exactly what will happen—but first we have to find them.'

'I wish you good luck,' Justin said. 'Lucinda is in a delicate situation, therefore I can only do so much to help in this investigation. I fear that most of the burden must fall on you, Andrew—though you may call on me if necessary.'

'I wish Lucinda a safe confinement when the time comes and congratulate you,' Andrew replied with none of the pain the announcement might once have caused him. 'You should take care of her and leave this business to me. I shall call on you only if I need you.'

'Lucinda comes first with me—but I feel responsible to Mariah in a way and will do all I can to recover her. I shall send to London for another agent to help in the search.'

'I already have a good man on the trail, but we need as much help as we can get,' Andrew said and his expression was both grim and determined. 'I am fairly certain that Mariah will not be found locally. This rogue will have her somewhere secure by now. We had a chance that we might find them at an inn nearby, but too much time has elapsed now. You will, of course, let me know if you hear anything?'

'Of course. I wish you good luck in your search for Jane,' Avonlea said. 'If you find her, you may also find Mariah.'

'It is my fervent prayer that we shall find them both—though I think not together, for I am certain they were separated.'

Andrew's face was set as he made his farewells and left Avonlea's house. He knew that it might be impossible to find Jane. She might even be dead. Mariah was probably being kept safe in the hope of her fortune. Andrew drew some comfort from that, but his feelings were in such turmoil that he hardly knew whether he was more concerned for Mariah Fanshawe or for his sister.

Something told him Jane might have escaped her captors and if that were the case his highly independent sister might even now be on her way home.

If only that were so. He would then be able to concentrate all his efforts on finding Mariah.

Chapter Three

'It is a pity your caretaker did not have a horse you could borrow,' Jane said as they stopped by a river to let George's horse rest and drink. Dusk was falling softly over the countryside, hiding the contours of roads, houses and barns, making her feel they were alone in all the world. 'Or perhaps you did not trust me to ride alone?'

George looked at her in silence for a moment. 'I thought you had agreed to trust me?'

'We could have travelled faster with two horses.'

'Yes, that is true—but Mrs Muffet would have wondered how two gentlemen had arrived with only one horse between them. I wished to protect your reputation.' His eyes seemed to burn into her, making her tremble inwardly. 'Will you not give me your trust, Jane?'

Jane looked at him in silence. Her mind wavered between trusting him and understanding his predicament, and condemning him for his part in the affair. She sighed, because she was stiff, her ankle had begun to ache again and she was tired of being so uncomfortable. The thought of her home and her brother made her eyes prick with tears. Andrew would be out of his mind with worry.

'My name is Jane Lanchester,' she said as George turned away and then handed her a flask of water he had brought with them. 'We live at Hillcrest. It is a lovely Queen Anne house not ten miles from the Avonlea estate. My brother is Lord Andrew Lanchester. Blair was my mother's maiden name.'

George smiled at her, and once again Jane felt that odd pull at her heart. She ought not to feel anything for a man she did not know and was not sure she could trust, yet there was something about him and their situation that made her want to let down her guard.

'Thank you. I shall try to send word to your brother, tell him not to worry.'

'Why do you not confide the whole in Andrew?' Jane asked and rubbed at the back of her neck tiredly. 'He would be grateful to you for helping me and he might be able to help you find Blake.'

'I think it more likely he would call the magistrate and have me arrested. In his shoes I should certainly do so. Besides, I still believe you should remain hidden, Miss Lanchester. Should Blake discover who you are and where you live, you would be at risk…'

'Yes, I know the risk.' Jane frowned. She bit her lip. 'I suppose he would kill Andrew as well if he stood in his way. I had not thought of that—it would be my fault for becoming embroiled in this affair. How much damage one might do without intending it.'

'It is a sobering thought, is it not?' George looked grave. 'Perhaps now you begin to understand what compelled me to do something I should not otherwise have contemplated.'

'Yes, perhaps I do a little,' Jane agreed. Her heart pounded, for she was very much affected by him in a way she hardly understood. Surely she could not be attracted to a man she ought to despise? She drank some of the water and splashed some on her face. 'Have we far to go?'

He looked at her in concern and once again her heart raced. 'You are tired? I have pushed you too hard, but I am concerned that Blake may be looking for you—or us. I think he may suspect me of helping you.'

'I am sorry. I have caused you a great deal of trouble. I should have stayed out of it, as you told me, and looked for help after they took Mariah.'

'You thought only to help someone in distress. It was brave of you, Miss Lanchester—but reckless.'

'Andrew would say exactly the same.' Jane felt rueful. 'I know I am at fault. I have always acted first and thought after. My brother has scolded me for it many times. Had you not had to worry about me, you could have been looking for Mariah. You might have found her and rescued her by now.'

'It is not as easy as that,' George said. 'This situation is hardly your fault, Miss Lanchester. I have to locate Blake and then follow him without being seen. My chances of success are slim, because he will be on his guard—but I do know some of the places he likes to visit. He is often at a rather sleazy gambling hall in London. I may look for him there first.'

'You intend to leave me with your nurse and go to London?'

'You look alarmed. You should be safe enough with Martha. I cannot stay to protect you if I am to search for Lady Fanshawe.'

'No, of course not.'

He was right, of course he was right, but she was somehow bereft at the thought of being abandoned with a woman she did not know. For a moment her heart sank, then she thrust the unworthy thought from her mind. She had no need of a man to help her. Had she not made up her mind long ago that she would be independent and live her life as she pleased rather than be beholden to a man, who would inevitably ill use her and break her heart? How foolish she would be to allow her situation to make her weak.

'Come, we should go on. It is not far now.'

George held out his hand to her. Jane took a step towards him. Her foot slipped on a stone buried in the grass and she stumbled. George caught her and held her to him for a moment. He looked down at her.

'Are you ill? I have been thoughtless. You were knocked unconscious. You fell and hurt your ankle and we have ridden all day. I do not think another lady of my acquaintance would have put up with so much. Forgive me.'

Jane gazed up into his eyes. For a moment she felt weak and vulnerable, close to the tears she had been suppressing. He hesitated, then bent his head, his lips brushing her brow. The caress comforted her, though she ought to have rejected it. Instead she wanted to cling to him. Resisting the urge, she closed her eyes, fighting her tears, then looked up at him. She felt his arms close about her. He held her next to his body and his lips touched her hair; he stroked the back of her neck with his fingertips, his warmth comforting her. He did nothing to indicate a desire to make love to her; his embrace was one of comfort and reassurance, nothing more. For a moment Jane wished that she might stay in his arms for ever, but then she remembered who she was and why she was with this man and drew back.

'I am tired, that is all. Do not be concerned for me, sir. It is Mariah we should be anxious for. I shall be well enough when we can rest.'

'You are as much a victim in this as she,' George said and swept her up in his arms, hoisting her into the saddle before mounting behind her. His arms went about her, holding her close to him. 'Lean against me. Another hour or so and you can rest in Martha's cottage. She will take good care of you.'

'Thank you,' Jane whispered, her throat tight. It was ridiculous to feel like weeping. She was so much luckier than Mariah. Instead of criticising and scolding George, she should be thanking him for his care of her. Her own reckless nature had brought her to this pass. Were it not for her gallant knight, she might be dead.

'What scrape are you in now, sir?' Martha said as she opened her cottage door to him some two hours later. 'Good gracious, what is the matter with the young lady?'

'She has fainted, I think,' George replied. 'She was very tired and she has suffered a terrible ordeal, Martha. Please take us in, for I fear she can go no farther this night.'

'As if I would turn you down, sir.' Martha opened the door wide. 'She can sleep in my bed tonight. I put fresh sheets on it this very day. You carry her up and I'll tend to her—and then you can tell me what this is all about.'

'Thank you. I shall be for ever in your debt, Martha dearest.'

'Stop that nonsense,' the old lady muttered. 'Up those stairs with you. I'll bring what I need and see to her. The poor girl looks as if she has slept in her clothes for a week.'

'Not quite that long,' George said ruefully. 'But it is not surprising that she looks exhausted, as you will understand when I tell you.'

He carried Jane up to the small bedchamber at the top of the stairs. The ceilings were low and he had to bend his head to enter through the door. The bedroom window was tiny with panes of thick grey glass and the room was sparsely furnished with just the bed, a chest of drawers and a wooden chair. However, there was a sweet, fresh smell and the sheets on the bed were spotless, as white as could be.

He pulled back the covers and deposited Jane carefully on the sheet, placing pillows so that her head rested comfortably. Hovering, he watched anxiously for her to open her eyes but they remained shut, and when he touched her forehead it felt hot.

'I think she has a fever,' he said as Martha entered. 'She said she was very tired, but I thought it was just the strain of what she's been through. Is she ill?'

Martha bent over her, placing a hand to Jane's forehead. 'She may have a fever. What have you done to her?'

'I have tried to help her. She was hit over the head by ruthless men, abducted and locked up. She escaped by climbing out of a window, fell from a tree and since then I have been rushing her here.'

Martha's wise eyes studied his face. 'You're not

telling me the whole truth, sir—but I shan't scold you yet. I'll hear the young lady's story before I pass judgement.'

'Will she be all right? I thought it was just a faint, but she is so hot. I should be most distressed if anything should happen to her.'

'I'll see that it doesn't. Get off downstairs. There's a stew on the hob. Help yourself. I'll see to her and then I'll tell you my opinion.'

George hesitated, then inclined his head. 'I'll leave her to you, Martha. I need to know she's safe. I have other things I should do.'

'She'll be safe enough with me.'

George nodded, a little smile on his lips. 'That is why I brought her here.'

He was thoughtful as he walked down the stairs. He was not quite sure why Jane had made such an impression on him, but he knew that her safety had become his first concern.

Martha bent over the unconscious girl. She began to bathe her face, then her neck, arms and hands with cool water. As her cooling cloth did its work all over Jane's body, the girl sighed and Martha smiled. She took away her soiled clothes and dressed Jane in a fresh nightgown that had seen better days, then ran a brush over her tangled hair.

'You look a little better, my lovely,' Martha said, though Jane still had her eyes closed. ''Tis nothing but a bit of fever you've got. I'll brew you one of Martha's special tisanes and by morning you'll be yourself again.'

Satisfied that the girl was not very ill, Martha left her to sleep and went down the stairs. Her one-time nurseling was at the kitchen table, eating a good part of her supper. She smiled her satisfaction, feeling pleased she had bothered to cook that evening, which was not always the case, for bread and cheese was her usual fare.

'How is she?' George asked, getting to his feet anxiously. 'She will pull through?'

'She has a little fever, but it will pass. Now sit down, finish your supper while I make a brew for her—and then you can tell me the whole story.'

'Yes, I shall, because you too could be in danger, Martha. I brought Jane here because I wasn't sure what to do or where to hide her—but I might have brought trouble on you.'

'I've seen enough trouble in my time and I dare say I can manage, but you'd best tell me the truth, Master George, because if you lie I'll know.'

'I don't want Jane to know my full name yet. She knows only that my name is George.'

'So it is, though not the name most use for you.' Martha frowned at him. 'Why have you been lying to the poor lass? I hope she is not in trouble because of you?'

'No, not exactly.' George sighed and raked his thick dark hair back from his face. 'I had better start at the beginning when Verity asked me to help her.'

'Ah, Verity is mixed up in this.' Martha frowned. 'I might have known. She was forever in a scrape when she was young and who did she ask to help her out? You've taken many a beating to save her, Master George.'

He smiled and shook his head. 'She is my sister. I love her—and after Mama died I had to protect her. Father was a bully—and now her husband is much the same.'

'Yes, well, I can imagine what she has been up

to,' Martha said. 'What I want to know is what it has to do with the young woman upstairs…'

Jane sighed and opened her eyes, looking into the face of the woman bending over her. For a moment she could not think where she was, but then everything came rushing back and she gave a little cry.

'Where is George? Is he still here?'

'No, lass, he had things to do that would not wait. He asked me if you would be safe and I told him I would look after you. He was happy with that and went off first thing this morning before it was light.'

'But I wanted to say goodbye. I never really thanked him for all he has done for me.'

'You'll have chance enough when he comes back, lass.'

'He is coming back?' Jane snatched at the hope and it eased the curious pain in her breast.

'He told me to say that he will be here in two or three days.'

'Oh—I thought he was going to London, but he could not travel so far in that time. I'm not sure where I am, but I know it is a long way from London and my home.'

'You are in Wiltshire, lass. We are but twenty miles from Alderbury.'

'Then I am some distance from my brother's hunting box, but not as far from help as I had feared. If I could reach Alderbury, I might be known for we visit often when staying at my brother's estate in this part of the country, though his family seat is near Avonlea and that is my home. I am not sure how best to get home—will George take me when he returns?'

'I don't know, lass. He said he had several things to do, but would be here in two days unless unavoidably detained. I don't know anything about London. I dare say he will tell you what he has been up to when he returns.'

'Yes, perhaps.' Jane gazed at her thoughtfully. 'I am sorry to be so much trouble to you, ma'am.'

'Nay, lass, call me Martha. I've never been ma'am to anyone. Some call me a witch, some call me Martha the wise woman, and some won't use my name at all. I do no harm to any, but there are those that fear me.'

'The tisane you gave me during the night helped me,' Jane said. 'I shall call you Martha, as George does—if you will permit it?'

'Yes, of course, lass. So what should I be calling you?'

'My name is Jane—Jane Lanchester.'

'Well, Miss Jane…what are we to do about this wicked rogue who has snatched your friend, then? Master George has gone to see what he can find out, but I doubt a rogue like that will be easy to find.'

'He could be almost anywhere.' Jane smothered a sob. 'He may harm her if he isn't stopped in time—and that will be my fault for delaying George. Had I not interfered he might have found her by now.'

'Mebbe and mebbe not,' Martha said. ''Twas a rash thing you did, Mistress Jane—but mayhap it was meant to be. Fate works in mysterious ways and it may yet turn out for the best.'

'What do you mean?' Jane sat up, her head whirling. 'How can what happened be a good thing?'

'I feel it in my bones,' Martha said. 'I'm no

witch, mistress, but sometimes I see things—and I can read the tea leaves. I read Master George's last night. He is in danger, there's no denying it—and so are you—but I saw good fortune in the leaves.'

'I pray you are right, Martha.' Jane closed her eyes and lay back on the pillow. 'I ought to get up. I am sure this is your bed and I have robbed you of a night's rest—but I feel a little dizzy.'

'There's no hurry, lass. I slept on the sofa last night and George had a blanket on the floor. I'll bring you something to eat and you'll feel better soon. Until then, you should stay in bed.'

'Thank you.' Jane sighed. She was too weary to argue and she felt tearful. George had gone without saying goodbye to her. Would he return?

It shouldn't matter. Now that he had left her she ought to be making plans to go home, but for the moment she did not feel well enough to make the attempt. Besides, if she did that, she might never see George again—and all contact with him would be broken. At least this way he might still help them rescue Mariah. Andrew would be worried, but perhaps George would keep his word and send her brother a message to let him know she was safe.

If she was safe! If George was right, Blake might still be looking for them. He might even turn up at the cottage.

'Please come back, George,' Jane whispered, and a tear slid down her cheek. 'Please do not leave me alone.'

She wasn't alone. She was with a very kind woman who had given up her bed for her.

Jane wiped the tears away with the back of her hand. She was not a foolish weak woman to go into a decline because a man had left her. Once before she had thought herself falling in love with a man she hardly knew, but she had heard him dismiss her as that 'plain-faced harpy'. He'd declared to a friend that he wouldn't take her if she had twenty thousand a year.

That man's cruel words, even though spoken in jest, had hurt her deeply. She'd decided then that she would not lay herself open to similar hurt again and had declined all attempts to draw her into another London Season. She would be very foolish to let her heart be touched by a man who had helped abduct her, even if he been kind to her. Jane wasn't even sure that he would keep his word to return for her.

She would stay here for two days, but, if George didn't return by then, she would find her way home somehow.

Jane was able to get up later that day. She went down to the kitchen to sit with Martha, refusing to use the best parlour even though she was invited.

'I do not intend to sit around wasting my time until George returns,' she said. 'Today I shall just sit quietly, but tomorrow I could help you— if you would find me some work.'

'In the morning, I must collect herbs and roots that I use for my cures,' Martha said. 'When I return I shall need to wash and chop them before I can make my recipes. You could help me with that if you choose.'

Jane thanked her. She was determined to earn her keep somehow, and after they had eaten their evening meal, helped to clear away and wash the dishes. Martha insisted that she take the bed again when it grew dark and since she would not be persuaded to let Jane take the sofa, she was obliged to give way.

She was wearing clothes Martha had provided. The much-washed linen gown fitted her well enough, though it was far from fashionable and had probably been Martha's when she was young. Jane smiled to herself as she donned a rather too-large nightgown and slipped between the sheets. She was tired and went to sleep almost at once, though when she woke there were tears on her cheeks.

In the morning she went down to find the kitchen empty. Martha had lit the fire and there was a blackened copper kettle steaming away on the hob and some warm bread rolls wrapped in a cloth. Jane fetched butter from the pantry and spread one of the rolls, smearing it thinly with honey. It was clear to her that Martha lived frugally and she made up her mind that she would find some way of repaying the woman's kindness once she was at liberty to go home.

It occurred to her that there was nothing to stop her leaving the cottage and making her way home right away. Yet she had no money and, though her ankle had almost completely recovered, she might have to walk all the way home. On horseback she could reach Alderbury within a few hours, but on foot it would take much longer. Besides, she would be alone and she could not be certain that Blake did not have men looking for her.

Her own situation was comfortable compared to Mariah's. Jane felt anxious and guilty as she thought of her friend. She wished she might do something to help Mariah, yet she believed the duke would be searching for his ward. Jane knew the name of her abductor, but there was no further clue she could give them. The only person who might be able to help was George. She just had to hope that he would return and bring news of her neighbour.

'What do you make of this?' Andrew asked and showed Avonlea the brief letter he had found on his return home after a day of fruitless searching. 'It is signed by someone who calls himself a friend...'

Justin took the note and read it aloud.

Your sister is safe for the moment, but she might be in danger if she returns home. The devil that kidnapped her and Lady Fanshawe is ruthless. He wants Lady Fanshawe's fortune and means to have it and her. When I have news I shall send word. There is no need to be anxious for Miss Lanchester at this moment. She sends her love and asks you not to worry. A friend.

'I'm damned if I know,' he said, his brow furrowed. 'Is it a trick to put us off the scent, do you think?'

'If Jane trusted this fellow, she would try to get word to me.' Andrew looked thoughtful. 'It seems as if our theories were correct. It is Mariah's money this rogue is after.'

'Who do you imagine sent you the letter?'

'If I knew, I should be out looking for him,' Andrew said. 'If I have correctly interpreted this message, he has Jane hidden away somewhere while he looks for Mariah.'

'Why should he do that?' Justin scowled. 'If he has information about this affair, he should come to me. He probably thinks to extort money from me by hinting that he can help when he has had both Mariah and Jane captive all the time. I heard from Mariah's trustees this morning—they have still heard nothing. I do not think the rogue intends to ransom Mariah. He plans marriage or—God knows what he will do.'

'Anything is possible,' Andrew agreed. 'Yet I think this letter well intentioned. I shall continue the search for her, though at the moment I have no idea where to look next. I am going to pay a visit to my hunting box in Wiltshire. I shall visit the local magistrates and post some missing-person notices in the vicinity. I doubt she will be there, but I've had no luck locally and there is a matter of business I must attend in Alderbury. It cannot hurt to widen the search and if I sit here and do nothing I shall go out of my mind.'

'Be careful with those foxgloves,' Martha said. 'Scrub your hands thoroughly before you touch your lips. They have healing properties, but are poison if the juice is swallowed in large doses.'

'Yes, I have heard that,' Jane said and smiled.

'My nurse dragged me off to wash my hands when I had been picking them as a child. She was worried that I might be ill and gave me something that made me sick just in case.'

'No doubt she was worried that she would be blamed if anything happened. Children are often a worry to their nurses.'

'What are you making?' Jane asked, looking curious as Martha ground seeds and juices into a pulp.

'It is a potion to treat the hind leg of a cow,' Martha said. 'Most people cannot afford to pay the apothecary to treat their animals. I charge nothing for what I gather in the hedgerows, but sometimes a grateful farmer or the mother of a sick child will bring me a gift of food.'

'What would make your life easier here, Martha? I doubt you have much need of money. You seem to grow or scavenge for all you need in the fields.'

'I had a cow until it died of old age,' Martha said and gave her a wry smile. 'Milk is a luxury for me these days—cheese, too.'

Jane nodded as she finished chopping some

horseradish roots and stored the pieces in little pots. She was reaching for the cloth to wash the pine tabletop when she heard the sound of a horse outside.

'Go upstairs until I call you,' Martha said. 'It is best to be careful just in case.'

Jane went through the door that shut off the staircase. However, she was no more than halfway up the stairs when she heard Martha call to her and ran back down, her heart racing.

George was standing in the kitchen. Until this moment she had not realised how tall and strong he was—or how much she'd missed him. Her heart pounded and the palms of her hands were warm and sticky.

'You did not go to London then?'

'No. I must do so soon, perhaps tomorrow. I went to find someone—someone who knows Blake better than I do. He gave me a few ideas. I now know where he lives—and at least one place he frequents that I did not know of before.'

'Do you think he has Mariah there?'

'I cannot say, but I intend to find out tomorrow.'

'Why do you not tell her guardian?'

'Who is that?'

'Well, before she was married the Duke of Avonlea was her guardian—but there are other trustees now. Still, I think the duke would be the proper person to approach. I am certain he would be reasonable and listen to your story, for he is a most correct man.'

'Then I may do so as soon as I have news. As yet it may be a wild goose chase. And Blake still has something of mine. I need to find it before I give him up.'

'That is selfish and wrong, sir.' Jane sent him a hard look. 'Whatever hold this rogue has over you it cannot be as important as a girl's life.'

For a moment anger flashed in his dark eyes and his mouth tightened. She saw the way his fists balled at his side, but he answered her in the same calm tone.

'As I told you before, Jane, if it were just me that would suffer, I would give him up now— would have done so before this. Please believe me, I am as concerned for Lady Fanshawe's safety as you are.'

'Why do you not tell her the truth?' Martha

asked and looked up from her work. 'You are too loyal sometimes, Master George.'

'Hold your tongue, Martha,' George said sharply. 'You will please keep your opinions to yourself.'

'You're a fool to yourself—and the lass is right. A woman's life is more important than—' Martha broke off as he looked at her and turned back to her work.

'You still have no idea where Mariah is being held?' Jane asked to break the tension. It would do no good to make him lose his temper.

'No, Miss Lanchester, I do not,' George said and looked her in the eyes. 'I have sent word to your brother that you are safe for the moment.'

'I cannot stay here much longer,' Jane said. 'Surely Blake will have given up looking for me by now?'

'Perhaps.' George appeared doubtful. 'I should like to talk to you alone, Miss Lanchester—if you would take a walk out with me?'

'Yes, of course.' Jane looked at her hostess. 'May I borrow your shawl, Martha?'

'Yes, of course, lass. 'Tis mild enough for the

time of year, but you're welcome to borrow it. I'm nearly done here. I'll be cooking a rabbit stew for our supper, but it will not be ready for three hours so you've plenty of time for your talk.'

'Thank you.' Jane turned to George. 'I think we do need to talk—and I should like a walk now that my ankle no longer hurts as much.'

He offered her his hand. After a moment's hesitation she took it and they went out of the kitchen door, walking through the vegetable garden to the lane beyond.

'I am very grateful to Martha for taking me in,' Jane said as they began to stroll across the open countryside towards a small wood. 'Yet I am certain my brother is searching for me, and he must be very worried. I think I should go home and take my chances. I cannot stay here for long. Martha has little enough food for herself and I am depriving her of her bed.'

George frowned. 'She is very proud. I have offered her money before this, but she refuses it.'

'She has no need of money. I think a cow, perhaps a sow in pig and some poultry. I shall certainly make her a present of the cow when I am home again.'

George was defensive, his mouth tight with annoyance.

'You make me feel that I have neglected her. In my defence I had been in the army until a few months ago—but, you are correct, I should have made certain she had all she needs.'

'As you say, she is proud and would not accept charity, but she has looked after me and I hope she will accept my gift.'

'I shall make certain she is able to survive the winter without hardship,' George said. 'Thank you for drawing my attention to her needs, Miss Lanchester. It was not intentional neglect.'

'I dare say you have had a great deal on your mind.'

'Yes, more than I wished for when I sold my commission,' he admitted ruefully. 'I had hoped for some peace and time to enjoy life, but it seems fate has decreed otherwise.'

They had reached a stile. George gave her his hand to help her over. As she came down the other side, she caught her heel in the hem of her dress that was slightly too long and fell. George moved swiftly to catch her. For a moment he held her close to his body.

Jane glanced up at him. She was not surprised when he lowered his head and kissed her. Something had been growing between them since that first night. His kiss was sweet, his lips firm and yet tender. He smiled ruefully as he released her. She found herself responding without reserve despite all her doubts. When he released her she felt sorry and wished she might cling to him, stay in his arms for ever.

'That was foolish and reprehensible of me, Miss Lanchester. I am in too much trouble to indulge in a flirtation and at the moment the future is uncertain.'

'It was a moment of madness, nothing more,' she excused him with a smile, though her heart had raced madly and she had felt something leap to life within her. 'I think I have been overly harsh with you, sir. You are not to blame for my abduction—and I have much to be grateful for. Indeed, had it not been for you, I think I should probably be dead.'

'I would not ask for gratitude. Yet I have no right to expect anything more.' George's look was thoughtful. 'Perhaps you *should* go home. Had Blake managed to follow us, I think he would have shown his hand by now. I should advise you not to walk alone and to stay indoors for a while, but I hope to discover Blake's whereabouts soon—and then...'

'If you manage to recover what you need, will you go to the magistrates then?'

'Blake must be stopped somehow. If Lady Fanshawe has been harmed in any way, her family will not rest until they have justice.'

'If you reveal your part in the affair, you may be arrested.'

'That is a chance I must take. After I have discovered Lady Fanshawe's whereabouts and done what I can to help her, I shall see that Blake is punished one way or another.'

'The person you contacted has no idea where Mariah might be?'

'No, I fear not. Blake told no one of his plans. The empty house we used for you was somewhere Blake knew of, but it was a spur-of-the-moment thing. He never had any intention of taking her there. Wherever she is, must be somewhere he believes quite secure.'

'Yet you do not think he has her at his home?'

'He is a devious creature,' George said and frowned. 'If he were suspected in this affair, his house would be the first place the magistrates would have searched. No, I am certain he has her somewhere else—somewhere no one would dream of searching. I think he may go abroad as soon as he has what he wants.'

'You think he may have taken her to the coast, to be near a ship?'

'It has crossed my mind that he may have planned something of the kind.'

'He might have taken Mariah abroad already, perhaps?'

'I am not sure he would want to run the risk. He will try to get her to agree to a marriage and then he needs a lawyer to draw up the nuptial agreement so that he can get his hands on her money.'

'If that is possible without her trustees' consent.'

George's gaze intensified. 'Could her trustees withhold the money, do you imagine?'

'I think it likely. My own fortune is slight, but even so, Andrew controls it until I marry or I am four and twenty.'

'A husband's rights will usually supersede a trustee's,' George replied. 'Avonlea could hardly refuse if his ward was in danger—or would he?'

'No, perhaps not, but he might demand Mariah's return. He could then fight Blake through the courts.'

George looked troubled. 'I think her life would truly be in danger if that were to be the case. Blake is a vengeful man. Unless he gets what he wants, he is unlikely to let Lady Fanshawe leave her captivity—and he might well decide she is of no further use to him.'

'You mean he would—kill her?'

'Let us hope that it does not come to that. Perhaps if I can discover her whereabouts, she may be released before Blake realises that he is unlikely to get what he wants from her trustees.'

Chapter Four

They walked in silence for a time. Jane felt shocked. She was more than ever convinced that she ought to return home and tell her story. She would not feel comfortable until she had spoken to her brother and the Duke of Avonlea. The knowledge that she had what might be vital information regarding Blake's appearance was gnawing at her conscience.

It was all so horrid and her nerves felt frayed. She knew she needed to go home and yet a part of her wanted to stay here with the man walking beside her.

'I shall take you home before I go to London,' George said, breaking into the silence that had grown between them. 'I think it may be for the best after all. However, I must ask you to promise that you will take—' He broke off and swore as they came in sight of Martha's cottage again, having walked in a semi-circle and come to it from another direction. 'There are horses outside the cottage. Stay here in the shelter of these trees, Jane. I must discover what is going on.'

She looked at him, feeling stunned and suddenly fearful. 'You think it may be Blake and some of his men?'

'I can think of no other explanation. Forgive me, Jane. I should have taken you home immediately. I thought you would be safer here, but it seems he has managed to find us here somehow.'

'If you could discover his home, he would be able to discover the whereabouts of your old nurse.' Jane touched his arm urgently. 'Martha is old and alone. Please go quickly. She may be in some trouble.'

'I shall try to get them away. Wait here out of sight until you see them leave.' He hesitated, then, 'If I am forced to go with them, you must make your own way home. It would be too dangerous for you to remain here now.'

'Yes, I shall,' she agreed. 'Please be careful,

George. I should not like anything to happen to you.'

'I wish—' He broke off, shaking his head. 'Forgive me. I must go. Remain here until they have gone—promise me?'

'Yes.'

George hesitated, then suddenly took her into his arms. This kiss was very different from those he had given her before, filled with a hungry, almost desperate need that made Jane cling to him.

'George...' she whispered as he let her go.

'Forgive me. It is impossible. In another life...' he said and turned away abruptly. 'May God protect you.'

Jane watched him stride away. She closed her eyes against the sting of tears. She wanted to call him back, but knew she must not. Blake was a ruthless devil and she feared for George if the part he had played in her escape had been discovered.

Drawing back into the trees, she watched him go inside the cottage. Nothing happened immediately and the minutes seemed to crawl by as she waited. What was happening in the cottage?

Was George all right? Had Blake harmed George or Martha?

She was on the point of disobeying George and going to investigate when the cottage door opened and the men came out. There were four of them, including George. She could not tell whether he was going with them willingly or under force. He mounted his horse and rode off with them. He did not glance once in her direction.

All the horses had gone. Jane ran as fast as she could towards the cottage. She was fearful that one of the men had been left behind to wait in case she returned, but when she entered the kitchen Martha was alone. The old woman was sitting in a chair by the fire and there was blood on her face.

'Martha!' Jane cried in distress. 'Did they hurt you?'

'They thought you were here and tried to make me tell them, but I refused to answer. They searched the house and then were about to hit me again when Master George came. He hit two of them and I thought they would kill us both, but then the leader told them to stop. He said it was obvious you were not here.'

'Why did George go with them?'

'He was ordered to at the point of a pistol,' Martha said. 'He went with them and that's all I can tell you.'

Jane saw that Martha's hands were trembling. She was clearly in shock and some distress.

'I will make some tea for you,' she said and knelt by Martha's side. 'Will you let me bathe your face?'

'Thank you,' Martha said. 'It is kind of you, lass, and I feel too shaky to do it for myself.'

Jane fetched water in a bowl and bathed away the blood. She found a balm on Martha's shelves and applied a little to the cuts and bruises on her face; then she poured boiling water into the large brown pot and stirred the leaves. When the brew was strong, as Martha liked it, she poured tea into a cup and sweetened it with honey, pouring another smaller amount for herself.

Martha drank her tea and then looked at her. 'You will have to go, lass. It isn't safe for you now. They could return at any time.'

'Yes, I know,' Jane said. 'George told me I must make my way home alone. I'll stay until the morning to make sure you are all right—then I'll go.'

'I think you should go now. I can manage alone. I'm used to looking out for myself—and I wouldn't want you to fall into that devil's hands if they should come back.'

Jane hesitated, feeling uncomfortable. 'I should have asked George for money…'

'I've no money to give you, but there's a pony in the field. It belongs to a farmer over the way, but he lets me use it for the pasture. Take it and send it back when you're safe. It is the best I can do for you, lass. You'll find a side saddle in me barn—it belonged to Miss Verity. She had it as a girl and I kept it for her.'

'Miss Verity?'

'Master George's sister. She came here a few times, kept her horse here until…but that's gone now. I've only the pony to offer you.'

'It is generous of you to do so much. I promise I shall return your pony.' On impulse, Jane kissed her cheek. 'I am so sorry for what happened to you. I should not have come here. George should have let me take my chances rather than put you at risk.'

'You were exhausted and ill when you came here, lass.' Martha caught her hand. 'I would keep you here no matter the risk, but now they know about this place they may come back.'

'Then I shall go,' Jane said, feeling emotional. She had not known Martha long, but she hated to leave her alone and in distress. Yet it was the way the old lady chose to live and there was nothing she could do to change things—though when she had her brother's groom return the pony, she would also send a good milking cow. 'Forgive me for being so much trouble to you.'

''Twas not your fault, lass. You can come and visit me one day when this business is over and done.'

'Yes, I shall,' Jane promised.

She was troubled as she went out to the barn and found the saddle that George's sister had used when she visited her old nurse. He had not mentioned he had a sister, but she could not help wondering if it was his sister he was protecting from Blake's spite.

Catching the pony was not easy. It came when she called, expecting food, but when she tried to put the saddle and harness on, the pony bolted. Three times she had to coax it back to her and eventually managed to put on the harness and then the saddle.

Glancing back at the cottage, she tucked the little packet of food Martha had insisted she take inside her shawl, then mounted the reluctant pony. She looked back at the cottage and saw Martha in the doorway; she lifted a hand to wave as she put the pony to a walk and then a trot.

Martha had told her to follow the high road, which was through the woods and just past the village.

'You'll see a sign for Alderbury before you've travelled more than a mile,' Martha said. 'I know you've no money, but if you ask for Widow Merry Martin in Alderbury she'll give you supper and a bed for the night. After that, you'll have to fend for yourself.'

'Will everyone know of her?'

'Go to the Three Crowns Inn. Ask for her there and the landlord will direct you.'

Jane was thoughtful. She had heard her brother speak of the Three Crowns. His hunting box was not too far from Alderbury and he visited often in the Season. She believed he had stayed there more than once and might be known. Jane thought it might be better to ask for a bed there. She could then send word to her home, which was across the border in Hampshire and no more than fifty miles or so distant as the crow flies. Andrew would come for her and pay the bill. However, she had said nothing of her thoughts, simply thanking Martha for her advice and left.

It was lonely riding the pony through the woods. Jane knew the beast had no real speed, though it was strong enough. She could not escape if Blake or his men pursued her, but she must just hope that George had managed to convince them he did not know where she was. Fortunately, Martha had burned her ruined gown under the copper and since she had slept in the old lady's bed there was no evidence that she had ever been to the cottage.

Jane felt angry that Blake's rogues had hurt Martha. She hoped that Blake and his evil cronies would soon be behind bars where they belonged. If they were ruthless enough to harm an old woman because she told them she did not know Jane's whereabouts, what might they have done to her if they had caught her—and what was Mariah suffering even now?

Her mind turned to George. She had no idea of his true identity or where he lived. No doubt he would forget her now that he had advised her to go home.

She might never see him again. Jane knew that she ought not to care. He might not be the rogue behind Mariah's abduction, but he was involved with the men who had planned it. She should put him from her mind. It was more than likely that he, too, would go to prison for his part in the kidnap. Yet she could not help the sensation of loss that hung over her as she followed the high road, branching off at the crossroads towards the ancient village of Alderbury. For the first time in many years she had let down her guard with a man she liked and he had seemed to feel something for her—yet his parting words had told her that he thought a relationship between them was impossible.

Why should that hurt? She hardly knew the man.

It was dark when Jane finally reached the inn she had been searching for. The light had faded soon after she left the forest road behind and in the gloom she had almost given up hope of finding the inn she sought when she saw the lights spilling into the dark street and realised she had found the Three Crowns. As she dismounted in the yard and gave the pony's reins to the young groom who came running, Jane glanced down at herself and realised that she did not look like Miss Lanchester of Hillcrest. Indeed, she had no bonnet, a dress that was too long and past its best, and a shawl that had worn thin with use.

Hesitating outside the back door of the inn, Jane wondered if she had the courage to walk inside and ask to speak to the landlord. She must look a fright and she might be turned away if she explained that she had no money. She took a step towards the door just as it opened and a man came out. He stood full in the light as he looked about him and Jane's heart leaped as she recognised him.

'Andrew…' she cried and ran towards him. 'Oh, Andrew—I am so glad you are here. I was going to ask if they would send you word, but now you are here and I am saved…'

'Jane?' Her brother's face registered disbelief, astonishment as he saw the state of her, then relief. 'I have been out of my mind with worry. Where have you been? What happened to you?'

'Andrew…' Jane choked, tears trickling down her cheeks. 'Please do not be cross. I've ridden miles on a wretched pony that refused to go above a trot. I'm tired and cold and worried to death. Will you please take me to your hunting lodge before you scold me?'

Andrew put his arms about her, holding her pressed to his chest. 'I may scold you later, dear one, but for the moment I am just glad to have found you. I believed the men who took Mariah Fanshawe had abducted you.'

'Yes, they did, but someone helped me get

away.' Jane wiped her face with the back of her hand. 'I'll tell you everything, Andrew—but can we please go home?'

'I'll hire the landlord's chaise,' Andrew said. 'My horse can stay here for the moment. You can't ride in your state and I didn't bring my own carriage.'

'Why are you here? Did George tell you where to find me?'

'Who is George?' Andrew frowned. 'I came down on business. If you want the truth, someone has made me an offer for the lodge and I am of a mind to sell.'

Jane was stunned. 'But you love to hunt with the Wiltshire crowd.'

'I have friends who will invite me for a few days' hunting should I wish it. Besides, I have always lived well from my income and investments, but have little spare capital lying idle. I thought I might have need of a cash sum.'

'You thought a ransom might be asked for me?' Jane frowned. 'I know too much. He couldn't have risked it—no, he would kill me if he got the chance.'

'Are you speaking of this fellow George?'

'No, someone very different. He is a dangerous man, Andrew.'

'Do you wish to tell me what you know?'

'I shall tell you when we are home. Also, we should speak to the Duke of Avonlea as soon as possible.'

'I'll send word as soon as we are home,' her brother said. 'You will go to bed as soon as we're home, Jane. There's nothing to be done tonight that will not keep for the morning.'

'What do you mean? Mariah is still being held hostage.'

'Yes, I know, but the duke received a letter yesterday afternoon telling him she is safe and will remain so if he signs the release for her fortune.'

'Avonlea is not her guardian, but he must think it. George said he would—'

Andrew looked down at her in the light of the lamps hanging above the inn door. 'Who is behind this, Jane? How did you manage to escape—and who is George?'

'Take me home and I shall tell you everything.'

'Of course, you must be so tired. You may tell me when you are ready.'

'He was one of the men who abducted us,' Jane said. She had bathed and was dressed in a soft pink wool wrapping gown, sitting before the fire Andrew had lit in her private sitting room. 'No, do not look so angry. You do not understand. George was blackmailed into helping them—and he believed Mariah willing. When he realised it was abduction and not an elopement, he planned to help her escape as soon as he had the chance— but I pretended to be her and they decided to take me, too. I was unconscious when they separated us and I do not know where they took her.'

'Jane, why did you do such a foolish thing?'

'I have no fortune. I thought they would soon release me when they realised it—but it was foolish. I did not realise what a ruthless man Blake is then.'

'Who is Blake? Not this George fellow, I take it?'

'No, they are very different.'

She sipped her wine and lifted her eyes to his.

'I know I was foolish. Mariah was hurt and I didn't stop to think. They tried to bundle her into the carriage and I attempted to stop them. I pulled the mask from one man's face and I saw another's eyes—the most unusual eyes, Andrew, for they were different colours. I fought them and told them they would hang if they persisted in their wickedness. Then someone hit me over the head and I knew no more until I woke up in the bedchamber of a neglected country house.'

Andrew nodded. 'Yes, I found the house and signs that someone had been there. How did you escape and where have you been since then?'

She set down her wineglass and told him the whole story, up to the point where she'd ridden out alone from Martha's cottage.

'George went with them after they found us, because he had no choice. I stayed hidden until after they left, then went back to help Martha, but she sent me away, because she was afraid they might return. The pony is hers—at least, it belongs to a farmer who lends it to her—and she needs a cow, Andrew. I must buy her a good milking cow. She looked after me when I had a fever.'

Andrew was glaring at her. Jane drew a shaky breath.

'Why are you looking at me like that?'

'You never think,' Andrew said in a scathing tone. 'Had you been sensible you might have been left to return home in safety. We might have found Mariah before this—and you should certainly have come home as soon as that rogue left you alone at the cottage. You were not a prisoner, so why did you not leave immediately?'

'My ankle was still sore. Besides, George thought I was safer there than here.'

'Nonsense! Do not tell me you believed him?'

'You don't know what kind of a man Blake is, Andrew. George saved my life. I trusted him— and I didn't know what to do. He said he needed time to find something before he went to the magistrates.'

'I dare say he wants time to make his plans before he runs off overseas. The man is a blaggard and deserves to hang with the rest of them.'

'That isn't fair,' Jane protested. 'If it were not

for George, I might be dead. He lied to protect me. He led the others away from the hut where I was hiding, then came back for me later. He bound my ankle and found food for us—and then took me to Martha's cottage. I had a fever because I was exhausted and—' She broke off, looking at him in distress. 'George isn't like Blake and the others. Please believe me. I don't know what hold that evil man has over him, but he is trying to find Blake's hideout—and Mariah. I am sure he will rescue her or send someone to find her as soon as he locates where she is being held.'

'He should have come straight to us,' Andrew said and looked grim. 'All this time has been wasted—and you should have had more sense than to allow him to blind you to the truth.'

'He has not harmed me, Andrew.' Jane looked at her brother reproachfully. 'I know you are angry, but you might be a little pleased to see me.'

'Of course I am pleased to see you.' Andrew swore under his breath. In his fear for Mariah, he was forgetting Jane's ordeal and blaming her for something that was not her fault. What kind of a brother was he? Mariah Fanshawe was hardly his concern, yet the thought of her in danger made his stomach clench with fear. 'I'm sorry. I do understand that you were trying to protect your friend—and I accept this George fellow helped you, but he is still guilty of abduction and that is a hanging matter. Unless he comes clean and helps us to find Mariah alive and unharmed…he may well hang with the others when we catch them.'

'Supposing you don't find them?'

'We have to find her. Avonlea has no power to release her fortune, only her trustees can do that. Besides, I doubt he would give way to blackmail. Avonlea is very angry, and I cannot blame him.'

'Mariah is more important than the money, isn't she?'

'Of course she is,' Andrew said, 'but if what you say is right, I fear for her life.'

Jane closed her eyes. 'I feel myself so much luckier than Mariah. No matter what you say, Andrew, George saved my life. I shall always be grateful to him.'

'Well, for that matter, I suppose I am grateful for what he did,' Andrew said. 'I've been out of my mind with worry. As for Justin Avonlea—I think he is at the end of his patience.'

Jane looked at her brother anxiously. It was unlike him to be so short with her.

'Are you in some trouble, Andrew? Something that has nothing to do with this business of the abduction?'

His gaze narrowed. 'Why do you ask?'

'You've been to Paris on some business for the regiment and you spoke of needing money. Was it only for my ransom if one were demanded? Surely we could have raised a loan?'

'How well you know me.' Andrew looked rueful. 'Yes, I may need money for something else. I am not in trouble, but a friend of mine may well be. Do not ask for more details, Jane. I am not at liberty to give them.'

'Then I shall not ask,' she said and rose to kiss his cheek. 'Think carefully whether you truly wish to sell, dearest. I shall see you in the morning.'

'You can tell me nothing more?' Justin Avonlea sighed and looked at Jane wearily. 'If I am being obtuse, you must forgive me. I feel responsible for Mariah's safety even though I am no longer her guardian. Lucinda is fond of her and believes that Mariah wished to tell me something concerning a fortune hunter. Had I listened to her, this might have been avoided. I find no fault in your actions, Miss Lanchester. You acted bravely, if rashly, and if we could find the man who helped you, we might have a chance of discovering Mariah's whereabouts.'

'Forgive me. I know nothing about him, other than what he told me,' Jane said and gave him an apologetic look. 'I am so very sorry for what happened to Mariah, sir. You have my word that if I remember anything more I shall inform you immediately.'

Justin paced the small parlour, then turned to look at her and Andrew.

'I may have to give into the rogue's blackmail and ask her trustees to release Mariah's fortune, which I imagine they must do if her life is in danger—but I shall need proof that she is still alive and unharmed.'

'George felt that Blake would most certainly

wish to keep Mariah alive. He may have used persuasion to force her to marry him.'

'Mariah is stubborn. She would not easily give in to persuasion or blackmail. I fear he may have grown tired of waiting and...' Justin shook his head as if the pictures his words conjured up were intolerable. 'I should have insisted that Mariah told me why she came to us. I should have known that she was in trouble.'

'No, you must not blame yourself,' Jane told him. 'Captain Blake—whoever he may be— was determined on abduction. He is the one you should be searching for.' Her eyes went to her brother. 'I think he must be a military man. You have not heard of him?'

'No, not that I can recall. However, I shall visit headquarters and make enquiries when we go to London, Jane.'

'You are thinking of going to London?' Justin asked.

'Jane's godmother sent her a standing invitation some time back,' Andrew replied. 'I intend to help in the search for Mariah. I have to visit headquarters and ask for extended leave—and I think Jane might be safer with Lady Mary.'

'I should prefer to remain here and help in the search for Mariah,' Jane said. 'There must be some way I can help. If I returned the pony and bought a cow for Martha, she might be persuaded to tell me where I could contact George.'

'Yes, that might be a good idea,' Andrew said. 'However, I shall do that myself. You will stay here and rest until I return, Jane.'

'You must promise me not to bully her. She helped me and those awful men treated her dreadfully.'

Andrew gave his sister a reproachful look. 'Do you imagine I would inflict pain on an old woman? I shall merely ask if she has heard from him or been troubled again. It is possible that one of those men let something slip—and if she understands that I mean George no harm, perhaps she will allow me to speak with him.'

'Perhaps,' Jane said doubtfully. Martha would never betray the man she had nursed as a child to a stranger. She might have given Jane a clue as to where she could contact him, but Andrew seemed determined that her part in the adventure was over. 'I doubt she will tell you anything, but there is no harm in trying. I still think you should be looking for Blake.'

'I shall do that, Miss Lanchester,' Justin said. 'I will post up to London to enquire. May I ask you to visit Lucinda before you leave? I must speak to my lawyers, for if I am to release even a part of Mariah's fortune there will be many papers to sign, but I hate to leave my wife alone. However, it is not something that can be done instantly. I may have to pay the ransom myself.'

'Of course I shall visit Lucinda. I dare say you have both been anxious.' Jane saw his agitation and moved forwards to touch his arm in sympathy. 'My instincts tell me that Mariah is safe, though in uncomfortable circumstances. You must not give up hope of her recovery, sir.'

'You are very kind,' Justin said. 'I thank you for your concern, but I shall not rest until she is found.'

With that he took his leave of them. Andrew looked at Jane after he had gone, his eyes narrowed.

'I know you dislike being left out of this business, but it is for your own safety. Those men may still be watching for you. It is best for Martha's sake and yours that I go alone to visit her.'

'Very well.' Jane sighed. 'I know you are trying to protect me, but I am involved in this whether or not you wish it, Andrew. Please thank Martha for me—but promise me you will not do something rash. You are distressed, but George deserves more gratitude than anger from you.'

'Yes, perhaps you are right. However, we need to find him or Blake if we are to rescue Mariah. Please promise me you will not stray far from the house while I am gone.'

'I promise. You will not forget Martha's cow?'

'I shall purchase one from a local farmer,' Andrew promised and smiled. 'It is a pity you were not a boy, Jane. An army life would have suited you down to the ground.'

Jane smiled, but made no answer as her brother strode from the room. She glanced around the comfortable parlour. It was good to be home and have all her things about her, but she felt a sense of loss that she could not quite explain to herself.

She was anxious for Mariah's safety, of course, but that was not the whole of it. No doubt she was being very foolish, but at the moment her life seemed rather empty and meaningless. Jane had always been content with her simple pleasures in the countryside: drawing, playing the spinet, embroidery, walking with her dogs, riding and entertaining neighbours. Suddenly, none of her usual pastimes appealed and she found herself staring into space, feeling oddly lonely.

There was no point in brooding over what had happened. She must simply accept that she was unlikely to see George again.

Perhaps it was for the best. Andrew would scarcely encourage a friendship between them. Jane would just have to accept that the whole thing was a regrettable incident she would do well to put from her mind.

'I am so glad to see you safely returned,' Lucinda, Duchess of Avonlea, said as they sat together in her parlour the next morning. 'It was so brave of you to try to protect Mariah and so clever of you to escape your captors. I am certain

Mariah would have escaped, too, if she were able, but she must be kept more closely than you were.'

'I am certain she would be. Blake only wanted her. I was just a nuisance. Besides, I had help. Without George I am not certain I should still be alive. I believe Blake might have killed me had I not got away when I did.'

Lucinda shuddered and pulled her shawl about her shoulders. 'I remember how I felt when I was abducted by that awful man who wanted to blackmail me. Had it not been for Andrew and Mariah…'

'Do not think about it, dearest. It was different for me, because I knew I was not the intended victim and I managed to escape.'

'The man who helped you—you have no idea who he really is?'

'No…' Jane hesitated. 'It is foolish, I know, but I liked him so much.'

'Was he a gentleman?'

'Yes, I am sure of it. He would not tell me why he was with Blake that day, but I know he was being blackmailed.'

'You really liked him, didn't you?'

'Yes.' Jane could not meet her eyes as she said, 'Do you remember asking my advice before you married the duke?'

'Yes, of course.'

'Until you met him you had no intention of marrying?'

'None at all.'

'What was it that made you change your mind?'

Lucinda hesitated, then, 'I hardly know—except that something in the way he looked at me made me feel my life would not be worth anything without him.' Lucinda was a little shocked. 'Surely... I mean, you could do so much better, Jane.'

'Could I?' Jane looked rueful. 'I once heard myself described as a plain-faced harpy by a man I thought I cared for. I fear that perhaps my way of speaking plainly may have made gentlemen who might have offered for me take me in dislike.'

'No, how could they? I know you are fiercely independent, Jane, but I am sure you could marry if you wished.'

'Perhaps, but I have gained a reputation for

being outspoken and, in truth, I've found few men that I would wish to marry.'

'Are you saying that you care for the man who helped you escape from your abductors?'

'I am not certain what I am saying,' Jane confessed and laughed. 'I dare say it is all nerves and I shall forget him within a week.'

Jane sat in front of her dressing table, brushing her long dark hair. Andrew had been gone for two days without sending her any word of his intentions. It could not have taken him that long to ride to Martha's, speak with her and ride back. Even if he had stayed at an inn one night to break his journey, he should surely have been back by now. Where was he—and what was he doing?

She was concerned lest he had discovered something and gone looking for George—or, worse still, for Captain Blake. He would do much better to wait until Avonlea returned from London so that they could search together.

Uncertain whether her concern was more for her brother or for George, Jane was about to retire to bed when she heard something rattle against her bedroom window.

She went to look out and saw a man standing just below her in the courtyard. Fortunately, the moon was bright and she was able to see his face.

'George—is that you? What are you doing here?'

'Jane?' He looked up at her. 'Thank God you are here! Are you alone?'

'The servants are in the house, but my brother is not here. Why?'

'Come down and help me. I have Lady Fanshawe safe, but she has swooned and I think she may have a fit of hysterics if she opens her eyes and sees a strange man.'

'Oh, thank God! I am coming. Wait for me…'

Jane threw on a warm dressing robe over her nightgown, easing her feet into sensible slippers. She ran quickly down the stairs and opened the side door that led out into the courtyard. George came to her immediately, his eyes searching her face.

'How have you been? Are you well?'

'I am well enough, thank you. Where is Mariah?'

'I brought her here on my horse, but she fainted.

I have left her in your summerhouse. I wasn't sure what to do—I dared not take her to the duke's house. He would ask too many questions.'

'Avonlea is in London,' Jane said and fled across the lawn to the summerhouse. George was just behind her as she pushed open the door and went in. The moonlight revealed the unconscious figure of Mariah Fanshawe lying on a cane daybed, which Jane often used on summer days when she wished to be alone. She bent over her, feeling for a pulse in her throat. 'She is still unconscious. We must take her into the house. Can you carry her—or shall I fetch help?'

'I can manage. The fewer people who know of this the better,' George told her. 'She was just about conscious when I snatched her and she understood that I was helping her, but she fainted and I had to hold her for most of the time we were riding here. I strapped her to my body so that she could not fall—but I fear she is ill.'

'What has that devil done to her?'

'He may have drugged her. She shows no signs of being beaten or assaulted, but she was certainly in a fever of some kind. She called me by her guardian's name and I allowed her to think it.'

George had gathered the unconscious girl in his arms. Jane preceded him as they walked swiftly back into the house and up the stairs.

'We shall take her to the guestroom next to mine. My godmother stays there when she visits and the bed is always kept aired.'

'I thank God for your good sense,' George said. 'Blake led me to her and I took her when he left her to have his supper. It was only as I rode away with her that I realised that I could not take her home. Avonlea would have me arrested.'

Jane had pulled back the top covers and he gently placed Mariah in the bed, her head resting on the pile of soft pillows. She gave a little moan and her eyes flickered, but did not open. Jane touched her forehead. It was hot and damp.

'The duke might be more grateful and more understanding than you imagine,' Jane said. She felt her cheeks grow warm as George's eyes went over her and she realised that she was not properly dressed. He must think her lost to all propriety. 'However, you did well to bring her to me, sir. She certainly has a fever. I shall send for a doctor and keep her here until she is well enough to go home.'

'Thank you.' George looked into her eyes. 'I do not mind for my own sake, but as you know someone else would suffer if my part in this was revealed. Blake would destroy the happiness of someone I care for in revenge.'

'You have not yet recovered your property?'

'No, unfortunately not. I had hoped to find the things I need, but I discovered Lady Fanshawe first and acted on impulse.'

'It was a good and noble deed,' Jane told him with a look of approval. 'I hope it will not bring retribution on your head, sir.'

'I do not—' George broke off as they heard the tread of a man's footsteps in the hall. Then the door opened and a man entered. 'Damnation, I thought you said you were alone?'

'Jane? Who is…?' Andrew's attention was drawn to the bed. 'Good God! Is that Mariah? How did she come to be here?'

'This gentleman brought her to me,' Jane said

with an apologetic glance at George. 'However, he wishes his part kept secret.'

'I must go,' George said. 'She is safe now. Goodbye.'

Andrew stared at him, moving swiftly to block his path. 'I suppose you are the man who helped abduct my sister—and then helped her to escape?'

George looked distinctly uncomfortable. 'Forgive me. I never intended harm to Miss Lanchester. I dare say she has explained the situation?'

'I should wish for a further explanation from you, sir. You will wait and speak to me in private. I wish to know more of—'

At that moment Mariah opened her eyes and gave a little scream of distress. Jane bent over her, smoothing her damp hair back from her forehead.

'You are safe now, Mariah,' she said softly.

Turning to look at Andrew, she said. 'Please fetch the doctor and send word to the duke and Lucinda so that she has no further need to worry. Mariah is safe now. George has risked much to help us. He is not your immediate concern now, Andrew. Mariah comes first.'

'Yes, you are right,' Andrew said and glared at George. 'Very well, I shall not prevent you from leaving. Just give me an idea of where I may find Blake—and your word that you will never come here again.'

George glanced at Jane, but she was busy bathing Mariah's head with a cool cloth and taking no notice of him or her brother.

'Very well,' he said. 'I shall tell you where I found Mariah—but Blake may be long gone. I do not know where he may have gone to ground, but he will be furious when he discovers Lady Fanshawe has been snatched and he may come looking for revenge.'

They went out of the room together, leaving Jane busy with her patient.

It was much later that evening, when the doctor had been by and given Mariah some medicine, that Jane had time to think and to realise that she still did not know who George really was—nor had she thanked him for what he had done for Mariah.

His visit had been so brief and interrupted by

Andrew before they'd had a chance to talk. Her brother had asked him not to come to the house again, which meant that Jane would probably never see him again.

A lump rose in her throat and tears stung her eyes, though she did not allow them to fall. Perhaps it was just as well. She could never have a future with George, even if he hinted he were willing—her friends and family simply wouldn't allow it.

Chapter Five

'I can never thank you enough for what you have done for Mariah, Jane.' Lucinda kissed her cheek. 'You have nursed her devotedly this past week or more, and now she is well enough to come home to her family. Justin is on his way home and he will be so thankful to have her safe again. We are so grateful for all you have done.'

'It was a pleasure,' Jane said. 'I am just sorry I could not do more. She might perhaps have been rescued sooner had I not interfered.'

'And she might still have been lost had your friend not found her and brought her to you. I think we have much to thank you for—and this mysterious George. He was wrong to be involved in the affair in the first place, but had he not been we might never have found Mariah alive.'

'She has not told us much of her ordeal,' Jane said. 'I think Blake meant to seduce her when he snatched her, but she fell ill and I believe he was frustrated in that intention. She seems much better today, though she is still very distressed, of course.'

Jane glanced towards Mariah, who was saying goodbye to Andrew. He had given her a posy of flowers from the hot houses, as he had every day since she recovered her senses and lay resting in her bedchamber.

Mariah came up to them then and offered her hand to Jane, who took it and held it to her cheek. 'I can never thank you enough, Jane dearest. Andrew told me that you persuaded that man to search for me. Had he not found me—' She shuddered. 'I am fortunate to be alive for I should never have married *him*.'

'Hush, you must try to forget what happened.'

'Yes, I shall,' Mariah said, a determined look in her eyes. 'But I shall never forget what you and your brother have done for me.'

'We have done nothing that you would not have done for me,' Jane said and kissed her cheek. 'We shall call and see how you are another day—shall we not, Andrew?'

'Yes, of course. Certainly. You are very welcome, Lady Fanshawe. You have my word that we shall not rest until the rogue who harmed you is arrested and punished.'

Mariah's pretty colour left her cheeks for a moment, then she raised her head proudly, turned and followed Lucinda into the carriage.

'How is Mariah today? You said that the duke was home. Did he discover anything about Blake when he was in London?' Jane asked the following afternoon when Andrew returned from a visit to Avonlea. 'Are you any closer to finding him?'

'We know that Blake was due for court-martial on a count of cheating at the card table and assaulting the wife of a fellow officer. He was cashiered, but disappeared before he could be tried. He is not received in decent society and may be in debt.' Andrew looked angry. 'Mariah has not told us much, but I think she knew him before her abduction. She told me that she blames herself for being careless. I think that must mean that he was an admirer at some time. Perhaps she fears she gave him reason to hope and the abduction was in part her own fault.'

'I am very sure it was not. You should not jump to conclusions,' Jane said and sighed. 'What will you do now? Are you at home for a while—or have you some other business?'

'I am not certain yet,' Andrew said, a closed look in his eyes. 'The affair that took me to Paris is not yet finished and I may be called on again.'

'I suppose you do not mean to tell me what that business is?' Jane saw the answer in his face and sighed. Her brother could be very secretive when he chose. 'Well, I shall not tease you. Do you know what Mariah means to do next? Will she visit her husband's relatives, as was planned before the abduction?'

'She said that she had been invited to go on an extended trip to Italy with Lord and Lady Hubert, who were great friends of her late husband, and thinks she may accept their invitation. Apparently, Lady Hubert has a weak chest and cannot stand the English winters—which means

Mariah would be away at least until late spring next year.'

'That is a long time.' There was an odd note in Andrew's voice, causing Jane to look at him intently.

'I thought you might be interested in Mariah yourself, Andrew?' His gaze narrowed and she sensed frustration or anger. 'Forgive me if I intrude. Perhaps I am wrong, but I thought you might care for her. You were much distressed by her disappearance.'

'Naturally I was concerned by the abduction of a friend,' Andrew said, glaring at her. 'However, even if I did feel something warmer towards her, there are considerations—problems that must first be overcome before I could ask any woman to marry me.'

'I see that you have something on your mind,' Jane said. 'Clearly, you do not wish to share your concerns with me.'

'It is not that I do not wish to. I am sworn to secrecy, Jane, and should not have told you so much. Please do not plague me, for I shall say no more on the subject.'

'Very well. I was merely concerned for the happiness of two people I care for.'

Andrew was silent for a moment, then, 'Avonlea says Mariah's recovery owes much to your influence over that fellow George—if that is his name. The very fact that he brought her to you shows he respects you. He refused to give me his true name, Jane. I believe he may be in some danger from Blake himself. If that rogue guesses who took her from under his nose, he may try to take revenge.'

'Yes, I believe you are right. I asked him to confide in you. Together, you might have tackled Blake much more easily.'

'Well, I would have pressed him if you had not ordered me to fetch the doctor.' Andrew looked thoughtful. 'You have seemed in low spirits since you came home, Jane. Is there something you have not told me? George did not… You were not harmed in *that* way?'

'If you are asking if I was dishonoured, the answer is no. George did something foolish for the sake of someone he cares for—but he is a gentleman and has his own code of honour. He did what he thought best—and who is to say he was wrong? Without his help both Mariah and I might have been lost.'

'I am relieved.' He frowned. 'Why are you so quiet and unlike yourself?'

'I have been busy looking after Mariah.'

'Is that all?' Andrew studied her. 'It would do you good to stay with your godmother. Why will you not be sensible and accept her invitation?'

'I shall think about it,' Jane said. 'I shall give you my decision this evening.'

'Very well. I must speak with my bailiff about some estate matters.' He hesitated, then, 'You know I am grateful for all you did here when I was serving in the army, Jane. If anything should happen to me, you would be well provided for, my dear sister.'

'Andrew! Why should anything happen to you?'

'It very likely will not, Jane, but I shall not lie to you. There are those that would like to see me out of the way—and I am not speaking just of your infamous Captain Blake.'

'You make me anxious for your safety.'

'I am well able to take care of myself, but perhaps you will understand now why I wish you to stay with your godmother. If I am called upon, I must go and should be anxious for your sake if I were away from home, perhaps abroad. I intend to do all I can to help Avonlea find the man who abducted both you and Mariah—but there is another matter that may become urgent at any time.'

'And of course you cannot tell me anything more. Very well, brother, I shall consider my godmother's invitation and give you my answer this evening.'

Sighing, she turned and went back into the house. It was an age since she had worked in her garden. The afternoon looked to be pleasant and she wanted to move some of the hyacinth bulbs, which had long since ceased to flower and would be best spread out from the clumps that had formed around the parent bulb. Now was the time to attend to these things before the cool of autumn turned to the bitter cold of winter.

Jane straightened up, putting a hand to her back. She had been on her knees in the garden for more than three hours, moving plants and bulbs to new beds. Her perennial borders were one of her chief pleasures and she had hoped her labour would lift this feeling of emptiness, but apart from the ache in her back she felt no different.

She stood, gathered her basket and tools and turned towards the house. Andrew had just ridden into the courtyard at the back of the house, his business with the bailiff done for the day. She lifted her hand and waved to him. He waved back and then turned to the groom who had come to take his horse just as the shot rang out.

A slight breeze on her cheek was all Jane felt as the ball passed her and buried itself in the trunk of a flowering cherry. She gave a cry and whirled round, looking for the source of the shot.

Andrew charged towards her as she stood transfixed, swaying, her face white with shock. He drew his pistol and fired in the direction of the tall shrubbery from whence the shot had been fired.

'Damn the rogue,' he said. 'I should go after him. Are you all right, Jane?'

'Yes. Go after him, but take care,' she whispered, then made a little murmur and fainted into his arms.

When Jane stirred and opened her eyes a minute or two later, she was lying on the sofa in their parlour. Andrew was bending over her and the housekeeper was waving a burnt feather under her nose. She coughed at the acrid smoke and sat up as her senses returned.

'You should have left me and gone after him,' she said. 'It must have been Blake. George said he might try to kill me if he discovered where we live.'

'You fainted. I could not desert you,' her brother said. 'Blake will keep for another day, Jane.'

'Yes, perhaps you should go to the magistrate and set up a hue and cry.'

'I have my own plans,' Andrew told her and frowned. 'One of which includes you, miss. Tomorrow I shall escort you to Lady Mary's house in London. You will be safer there. I am not going to take no for an answer. You will go to your godmother tomorrow, Jane—and there's an end to it.'

'Yes.' Jane sat up carefully. Her faintness had gone, but she still felt a little shaken. The shot had taken her by complete surprise. During her flight with George she had known Blake might try to kill her if he found her, but she had begun to feel safe at home.

Somehow Blake had found her. He might even know that George had brought Mariah to her—and he was clearly determined on revenge. She wasn't sure if the shot had been a warning or simply gone wide, but Andrew was right. She was not safe here. 'Yes, I may as well go. I shall be safer in London. Be careful, Andrew. Now you know how ruthless he is—he might kill you if you get in his way.'

'He may try,' Andrew replied grimly. 'If I find him, I shall not wait for him to shoot first, believe me. He is destined for the hangman's noose after what he did to Mariah—and to you. I thought to hand him over to the law, but after this...'

'Be careful, Andrew,' Jane said. 'You could end up in prison yourself.'

'At least that rogue would not bother you or Mariah again.'

'But you still have to find him.'

'Avonlea has hired a Bow Street Runner. I am going to do the same. While Blake remains at large he is a danger to both you and Mariah—perhaps to all of us.'

'George told me he will not give up the search.' Jane sighed. 'If only he had told me where we could contact him. He might know something that would help you.'

Andrew's gaze narrowed. 'I hope you have not formed an attachment to that rogue, Jane? I should never agree to anything between you.'

'Do not be ridiculous,' Jane replied too hastily. 'I hardly know him. If you will excuse me, I shall go up and pack. I just hope that my godmother will be pleased to see me without notice.'

She walked away from her brother, knowing that he was staring after her. Had she given herself away? She could not help thinking of George even though she told herself it was foolish. He would not wish to meet her again—and if he did so, it might bring him into danger.

Besides, she had long ago decided never to marry. Accustomed to living alone with only her brother's servants and meeting her friends as and when she chose, she had become very independent. It irked her that she must obey her brother and for the first time she considered whether she might do better to find herself a small house in Bath and take a companion. Andrew had never been dominant, giving her her own way in most things, but there was no doubt that his temper was shorter these days.

Jane's eyes stung with tears. She was over the shock of being fired at in her own garden, but the feeling of loss and emptiness would not leave her.

Perhaps in London she would find solace in making new friends.

'Of course I am glad to see you,' Lady Mary Sommers said as she embraced Jane. 'I am always happy to see you. Andrew said you had been distressed over a distasteful incident. You must put whatever it was behind you, my love. My friends are all from the very best society and you will suffer no unpleasant incidents in my company.'

'No, I am very sure I shall not,' Jane said and kissed her cheek. Andrew had clearly not told her of the abduction or the attempt on her life, for which she was grateful. It would be best not to have these things talked of. 'I am glad to be here and sorry I did not come before.'

'Well, no doubt you had your reasons, dear child. I know your first Season was a disappointment.'

'Well, if you recall, I developed a chill and had to go home.'

'You know I should like to see you settled, dearest. Andrew will marry one day and you will not want to be a maiden aunt staying in a house where you are not truly needed. However, you may always come and stay with me so there is no rush to form an attachment.'

'Even if there were haste, I could not conjure a suitor out of thin air,' Jane said and laughed. 'I have thought about the eventuality, you know. If Andrew decides to marry, I shall rent a house in Bath and take a companion to lend me countenance. I might do so sooner if I find someone suitable I can like.'

'Nonsense,' her godmother said and frowned. 'You are not in your dotage yet, Jane. You need a little town bronze, my love. I have no engagements for three days. Plenty of time to have some new gowns made—at least one and others ordered. You are attractive and your nature is lovely. I am certain you could find a suitable husband should you wish it.'

'Well, we shall not pull caps over it,' Jane said with an affectionate smile. 'If a man with good humour, a reasonable fortune and a pleasant face offers for me, I will engage to at least think about my answer for all of one hour.'

'You are a minx, miss,' Lady Mary said and laughed at the jest. 'If the gentlemen knew you as I do, they would fall over themselves to offer for you, Jane. I think you would make any man a good and generous wife. You have an even temper and get on with things without making a fuss. I do not know why you have not married before this, my dear. However, I have not given up hope of seeing you happy.'

'I am perfectly content.' Jane knew she was lying as she spoke. She had been content with her life, but that was before she had been abducted and rescued by a gentleman she could not dismiss from her thoughts.

'I think the gown you have chosen delightful,' Lady Mary said as their carriage drove back to Russell Square after a successful afternoon shopping in the very best emporiums. 'You were lucky to find those evening slippers, dearest. The colour is exactly the right shade.'

'Yes, I believe they will go very well.' Jane's attention wandered as she glanced through the carriage window and saw a man walking down the street. She stared very hard as they passed him. It was difficult to be sure, but her heart was hammering against her ribs because she believed it was the man she knew as George. What was he doing in London? He looked very different from when she had last seen him, his clothes fashionable and expensive. Weston's establishment must have made his coat, and he looked a man of fashion and stature. Could he possibly be the same man that had helped her escape from her abductors?

'What is wrong, Jane? You look shocked—as if you had seen a ghost.'

'No, not at all,' Jane replied. 'I thought I saw someone I knew, but I may have been mistaken.'

George—if it was he—had been escorting a very beautiful lady with blonde curls peeping from beneath her chip-straw bonnet. Who was she—and what was she to him?

Jane was aware of an unworthy feeling of jealousy. The lady was unknown to her, but she was certainly very lovely—and she had been smiling up at her companion in a confident and intimate manner.

She was being so foolish! Jane could not even be sure the man she had glimpsed was George—and even if it had been, he was at liberty to escort whomever he chose about town.

This was ridiculous! She had come to London in the hopes of forgetting her unhappy thoughts and the unpleasant incident that had started all this self-doubt. She had been mistaken and the man had been someone quite different. Why would George be in town? He had told her he intended to continue his search for Blake. Why then was he escorting a beautiful lady through the heart of Bond Street?

She made up her mind to put George and all the events of the past few weeks from her mind. It would be best for Jane to forget the man she had begun to like rather too well and concentrate on enjoying her stay in town.

'You look quite lovely, my dear,' Lady Mary said as they were preparing to attend a dinner given by the prince at Carlton House the next evening. 'You were a little insipid as a girl, if you do not mind me saying so—too quiet and easily pleased. Maturity suits you, Jane. Your character has developed and it shows. Besides, you are wearing rich colours, which suit you much better than the pastels you wore as a girl.'

'Thank you,' Jane said and laughed, amused that her godmother had thought her insipid as a girl. 'I was guided by a friend of my mother, who thought I ought to wear pastels. I was quiet because I had been told gentlemen did not like intelligent girls who had opinions of their own.'

'Absolute nonsense,' Lady Mary said stoutly. 'You must just be yourself, dearest. It is the only way. Any sensible gentleman will see what a treasure you are if he has eyes to see at all.'

'My dearest godmother, you make me feel so much better,' Jane said. 'I assure you I am looking forward to this evening, and I shall be myself for I cannot be anything else.'

Jane glanced around at the richly furnished room, with its ornate furnishings and magnificent chandeliers. It was the first time she had been invited to such a prestigious affair and the spacious rooms were overflowing with guests. Their dinner had been quite delicious and now everyone was looking forward to the entertainment, which consisted of a performance by both a tenor and a soprano of considerable fame. Some of the gentlemen were heading for the card room, where tables had been set up. There was no dancing that evening and Jane was preparing to take a seat to listen to the music when she caught sight of the gentleman she had glimpsed in Bond Street the previous day.

He was wearing evening clothes of a dark hue, with a pristine white shirt, and looked very distinguished. She had not been certain when she saw him briefly in the street, but studying him more closely now she was sure he was indeed George.

For a moment her heart raced. She had missed him more than she would admit to herself and her first inclination was to go to him at once—but of course she could not. It would be most improper of her. She must wait to be introduced or for George to come to her—but it was so very hard to see him and not be able to approach him.

What was he doing at an affair like this? As she watched, she saw that he had been engaged in conversation by Prince George himself. Jane frowned, because she could not understand how a man who was clearly welcome at important society affairs could have become embroiled in an abduction. What had he been thinking of to agree in the first place? He must have known how much he could lose.

'Who are you looking at, Jane?' Lady Mary glanced across the room and then smiled. 'He is rather distinguished, is he not? Lord George Marlowe—a very pleasant and good-mannered gentleman, Jane. I know his grandfather very well. His father died a year or so back in a fall from his horse, but the earl is still alive. He had three sons and Lord George is not in line for the title, though he will inherit a share of the earl's fortune—but he is wealthy enough in his own right. His mother was well connected and an heiress. If you could gain his regard, you would be fortunate indeed, my dear.'

Jane's cheeks felt warm. She had obviously shown her feelings too plainly.

'Please, Lady Mary, do not hint at such things. It is quite impossible.'

'Impossible? I do not see why. He is of an age to be looking for a wife, his wild days in the army behind him. I know him to be intelligent and a considerate brother. I dare say he would suit you very well.'

'Please, you must not.'

Jane's heart was racing. George—or Lord George

Marlowe, as her godmother had named him—was looking her way. For a moment the colour left his face and she knew he was shocked to see her. He was probably wondering if she would denounce him to his friends. She made a little negative movement of her head and sat down beside her aunt to listen to the music.

She was aware that he watched her throughout the next hour or so of music, her attention wandering from the beautiful tones of the soprano to thoughts of him.

When the interval was called and supper announced, Jane rose with her godmother and walked towards the splendid supper set out in the next reception room. She did not know how anyone could wish to eat after the lavish dinner they had been given earlier and moved towards the balcony, wishing only for a little fresh air. The prince was well known for keeping his rooms too warm.

'Miss Lanchester.' The voice made her turn swiftly but she was not surprised that he had come to her at the first opportunity. 'We must talk urgently.'

'Yes, my lord,' she replied. 'But not here—not this evening. Do not be alarmed. Lady Mary has no idea of who you are—at least, she does not know anything about what happened, other than that I was upset about something that happened at home. I have said nothing of you, nor shall I. Apparently, Lady Mary knows both you and your grandfather quite well.'

'Yes, that is perfectly true.' George met her challenging look. 'I should have told you the whole. Perhaps you would allow me to call on you tomorrow to explain?'

'I certainly think an explanation due, sir. My brother is searching for you in the hope of learning where he may find Blake.'

'Lady Fanshawe—is she well?'

'She has recovered in a physical sense, but her distress is inward and may trouble her much longer. She did not tell us much of what happened to her, though I understand she was not harmed other than by the foul drugs they gave her to keep her quiet.'

'Yes, I fear she was not well treated. I wish the thing had never happened, but regret is useless.'

'You will call tomorrow at eleven?'

'Yes, of course. Forgive me.'

'Tomorrow I shall decide whether you deserve to be forgiven,' Jane said, giving him a direct look. 'I should return to my godmother. She will worry if I am absent too long. I shall expect you in the morning, sir.'

'I shall not let you down, Miss Lanchester.'

He gave her a formal nod and moved on. Jane was swamped by disappointment. Though they'd been compelled to be formal with each other, was it just her imagination that George seemed most concerned that she would give him away? She had not felt that connection with him this time and felt its loss keenly.

Jane made her way to the dining parlour. She saw George enter a little later. He went to stand by the side of the beautiful young woman she had seen him accompanying in Bond Street, but did not glance her way. Was he deliberately avoiding making eye contact? She felt rejected, hurt.

Perhaps she had misunderstood that day—or perhaps he'd regretted that parting kiss.

A little niggle of doubt stirred in her mind.
What explanation could George give her—and
would he tell her the truth?

Jane had slept fitfully that night, tossing and
turning, caught in a nightmare. She woke suddenly, shivering and cold. In her dream she had
been abducted, but this time there was no George
to save her and she had been very frightened.
Since this was the first time she had suffered
from bad dreams over the abduction, she wondered what had brought things back so sharply.

It was impossible to sleep again so she rose
and sat by the window, watching the dawn light
strengthen. She was still there when the maid
brought her breakfast tray.

'Have you been awake long, miss?'

'Yes, for a while,' Jane said and smiled at her.
'At home I should get dressed and go walking
or riding alone, but in town I did not think it
advisable.'

'No, miss, I should think not. Is there anything more I can do for you? Would you like me to bring water for a bath?'

'No, just my usual water for washing,' Jane said. 'Please do not worry, Tilda. I am perfectly well. I had something on my mind.'

The maid nodded, set down her tray and left Jane to eat her breakfast. Jane poured the strong dark chocolate into a little bowl and sipped it, then buttered a warm roll and spread a little honey on it. At home she would have eaten her breakfast downstairs, but since her godmother never rose before eleven at the earliest it made too much work for the servants. A simple breakfast in bed was much easier for them than setting out the chafing dishes on the sideboard in the dining parlour.

When Tilda brought her water, Jane washed and dressed in a morning gown. She arranged her hair back in a simple knot at her nape, teasing out a tendril or two about her face. Satisfied with her appearance, she left her room and went downstairs to the parlour, attempting to read a book until the appointed hour.

* * *

'Lord George Marlowe,' Lady Mary's house-keeper announced, entering the parlour. 'He asked for Lady Mary, but said he would speak to you, miss. Do you wish me to remain in the room?'

'No, thank you. Lord George is a friend and quite respectable,' Jane said, a faint flush in her cheeks. 'I am two and twenty, Mrs Scott. I assure you there is no need to chaperon me with this gentleman.'

'Very well, miss. I shall show him in.'

The housekeeper gave her a dubious look as she turned to leave, which left Jane in little doubt that she had fallen in the good woman's opinion. However, it could not be helped, for it was imperative that they talk in private.

When George came in she was at the bow window that overlooked the street, gazing down at the garden in the square. She did not turn immediately when he entered and he coughed, before saying, 'This is rather awkward, Miss Lanchester. I dare not think what your godmother's house-keeper is thinking.'

'Perhaps that I am no better than I should be.' Jane turned to look at him. 'Fortunately, as I have no marriage prospects, a loss of reputation will not harm me too much, particularly as I prefer life in the country.'

'Have you suffered a loss of reputation?' George looked at her intently. 'I thought your brother and friends had kept things as quiet as possible?'

'Yes, they have,' Jane agreed. She raised her head, very much on the defensive. 'It was merely levity, sir. I have no wish to marry. Please, sit if you wish.' She returned to her former seat, which gave him the opportunity to sit if he chose. He remained standing, looking apprehensive and un-comfortable.

'I hardly know where to begin.'

'Please do sit down.' Jane indicated the large wing chair opposite hers. 'Now that the imme-diate danger is past, perhaps you might trust me with the truth about what hold Blake has over you?'

'He has some incriminating letters and other things.' George sat opposite her. 'Blake was once in my own regiment. At one time I invited him to shoot with me at my family home in the country—that was when my sister, Verity, met him. So I blame myself in part.'

'I do not quite follow.'

'The letters were written by Verity,' he explained. 'I was not at liberty to tell you before, but she has given her permission, though reluctantly. As I understand it, she had a brief affair with Blake after a quarrel with her husband. She did not know Blake's reputation—he had been due for court-martial, but found a way to wiggle out of it, even though he was dismissed from the army. When Verity realised that he was not the man she thought him, she broke off the affair—but Blake threatened to send the letters and an article of jewellery to her husband. If he does so, Markham will demand a divorce and Verity will be ruined.'

'Oh, no, how dreadful for her,' Jane said, feeling sympathy for the lady. 'You have my word that I shall never reveal one word of what you have told me. May I ask—was she the lady I saw you with last evening?'

'Yes, Verity was present last night.' George

sighed. 'She is a busy hostess and delights in the social calendar. If she were forced to leave London in disgrace, I think she would pine and fade away entirely. She loves her children and I fear Markham would forbid her to see them.'

'That is so unfair, though her husband has the right to be angry with her, of course,' Jane said. She leaned towards him and touched his hand. 'I understand completely why you felt compelled to help Blake, sir. You love your sister and wish to protect her, as any caring brother would.'

'Unfortunately, I have failed her,' George said. 'She has now received another blackmail letter. Blake is demanding twenty thousand pounds for the return of her possessions and the letter. Verity cannot pay and I shall have to sell land to find such a sum.'

'I thought you meant to discover where Blake was hiding and take back your sister's letters?'

'I searched for him, but after I rescued Mariah, he went to ground and I could find no sign of his whereabouts. Then I received a letter from Verity begging me to come to London.'

'I see...' Jane was thoughtful. 'My brother has

men searching for Blake and so has the duke. They are determined to bring him to justice. Would you consider meeting with Andrew and pooling what information you have? Perhaps one of you might have something that would lead to his discovery and capture.'

'Your brother made it clear that if I came near you again he would do his best to see me behind bars.'

'Andrew is sometimes hasty,' Jane said. 'I believe you would find the duke more reasonable. He was very grateful that you had brought Mariah back to us. Although she is no longer his ward in legal terms, he feels himself responsible for her safety and welfare.'

'If I could discover where Blake has gone to ground, I might also find the letters,' George said. 'Is your brother in town?'

'Not at this moment, but if I sent for him he would come. I know he has other business, but he wishes to see this unpleasant affair settled.'

'Very well, send for him,' George said. 'I shall not give him my reasons for being persuaded to join Blake—that information was for you alone,

Miss Lanchester. I did not wish you to think me a heartless rogue.'

'I have never thought that,' Jane said and smiled. She stood up and he rose to his feet. She moved towards him, gazing up into his face. 'If I can do anything to help you or your sister, I should count it an honour. I did not thank you sufficiently for rescuing both Mariah and me.'

'Miss Lanchester—' George broke off as the door to the parlour opened and Lady Mary entered. Jane felt her cheeks grow warm as she moved away from him. George bowed to her godmother and smiled. 'Lady Mary, forgive me for calling this early. I fear I have inconvenienced you and Miss Lanchester.'

'Not at all, my dear boy.' Lady Mary beamed and offered her hand for him to kiss. 'To what do we owe the pleasure of this visit?'

'Lady Markham is giving a small dinner this evening. She would very much like to invite you both, but fears that a late invitation may appear rude.'

'Not at all. I dare say she did not know I had my goddaughter staying. You may tell Verity that we shall be delighted to join you. We have a card party later in the evening, but were to dine at home. We can easily come to you and then go on later.'

'My sister will be so pleased,' George said and bowed to Jane. 'It has been delightful to renew our acquaintance, Miss Lanchester.'

'You know each other?'

'We met briefly some time ago,' Jane replied quickly. 'I was not sure last evening, but Lord George has reminded me.'

'Well, how pleasant this is to be sure,' Lady Mary said. 'Have you met Lady Markham?'

'I have seen her, but we have not yet met. I shall look forward to it.'

'I must take my leave,' George said. 'Once again, I ask you to forgive the early call, Lady Mary—Miss Lanchester.'

He bowed his head, turned and left the room. Lady Mary was silent for a moment, then, 'No wonder your attention was caught last evening, Jane. It is awkward when one cannot quite recall a face—though I do not think many young ladies would forget Lord George.'

'No, perhaps not,' Jane said and turned away, feeling guilty for lying to her. Her godmother's words were only too true. George—or Lord George, as she must think of him now—had scarcely been out of her thoughts since the night he found her in the hut. 'It was kind of Lady Markham to invite us, was it not?'

'Yes, though it is but a month since I last dined with her.' Lady Mary looked thoughtful. 'Lord George intended a longer stay in the country, I believe. He must have returned to town at his sister's request. I have thought something was troubling her of late—I suppose you know nothing of it, Jane?'

'If I had been given privileged information, I could not repeat it, ma'am.'

'No, you could not and I should not wish you to,' Lady Mary replied. 'I shall not ask you to break a confidence, though I may know more than you imagine. Yes, I see—things begin to make sense now.'

Jane wondered just how much her godmother did know of the affair, but she was not at liberty to discuss Lady Markham's predicament. Lord

George had told her in confidence, because he did not wish her to think ill of him. Was there something more on his mind? Jane suspected that she would have heard more if Lady Mary had not arrived when she did.

'Do they?' Jane smiled. 'Shall I send for some refreshments, ma'am? After that, I have a letter to write...'

'Oh, George—' Lady Markham looked at her brother in distress '—I wish you had not told her. What will she think of me?'

'I told you I must, dearest. Jane deserved an explanation,' he replied sternly. 'Forgive me, but I needed her to know the truth—to understand why I agreed to help Blake in the first place.'

It had shocked George to see Jane the previous evening. For a moment he'd thought he might be accused of his ill deeds before his friends, but then he'd known that Jane would not be so cruel. Even so, he had not been able to greet her naturally. After her brother had forbidden him to contact her, he had reluctantly decided that he must dismiss her from his mind. A resolution that was harder to achieve than he had expected. Jane was a remarkable young woman, very different from his sister and mother. Her cool independence had impressed him and he had felt a burning need to protect her, but when he'd ridden off with Blake that day he had believed he might die within hours.

It had taken a lot of swift talking to convince Blake that he knew nothing of her whereabouts. They had argued violently and George knew that the other man had come close to shooting him that day. He had survived because Blake thought he would not dare to speak out lest he lose both reputation and perhaps his life.

'I wish I had never met him!'

George's attention returned to his sister. He looked at her ruefully as she wiped her tears.

'That was my fault for introducing you. Had I known what a rogue he was, I should never have invited him to join us that autumn.'

'It was not your fault, George,' Verity replied and dabbed at her eyes with a lace kerchief scented with lavender water. 'I do not know what possessed me to become involved with him. I had discovered Markham's affair and we were at odds, but I should not have been drawn into a clandestine relationship of my own. This is all my fault.'

'No, dearest,' Lord George comforted his sister. 'You need not imagine that Jane would betray you. She is the bravest…the most sympathetic of women…'

'You care for her?' Verity's soft brown eyes widened.

'I hardly know Miss Lanchester—but, yes, I do care for her good opinion.' Lord George sighed. He was uncertain as to the depths of his feelings, though he suspected that they might be deeper than he knew. 'I dare say she thinks me an unprincipled rogue—but she would never betray me or you.'

'I have ruined your life as well as my own,' his sister declared a trifle dramatically. 'You will hate me. You cannot possibly pay such a huge sum. What shall I do? Markham will divorce me.'

'It may not come to that,' he said to comfort her. 'I am looking into my affairs to see how much I can raise. Blake may be reasonable—or I may be able to recover the letters. I should attempt it if I could discover where he has hidden them.'

'Would he not have them at his country house?' Verity said. 'It is little more than a cottage, really, but no more than an hour's ride from Markham's estate. It was where we met when…'

Lord George stared at his sister in disbelief. 'Why have you not mentioned this before? You knew I was searching for him, Verity.'

'I thought you knew he had a house in Devon.' She blushed and turned away abruptly. 'I was embarrassed to mention it and it slipped my mind until this moment.'

Lord George bit back the sharp remark. Had his sister felt inclined to tell him this, he might never have become embroiled in the abduction in the first place.

'If you will furnish me with more details, I shall pay Captain Blake a visit tomorrow.'

'I dare say he will not be there. His last letter hinted that he was in town and would contact me soon. Besides, the house is closed up and there is only a caretaker—which was convenient when…' Once again she was unable to continue.

'All the better. I intend to search the place and it may be easier if there is only a caretaker to deal with.'

'Supposing he is there—supposing he discovers you searching his house?' Verity gave a little sob of despair. 'He would kill you and ruin me. If Markham discovers the truth, it will be the end of everything.'

'Have you not considered telling your husband the truth? Perhaps it would clear the air between you. If you told him how miserable you were and swore it would not happen again, he might forgive you.'

'Please, do not ask me to do that,' his sister cried in alarm. 'You must help me, George. If I am disgraced, I shall kill myself.'

'Promise me you will not be so foolish.' Lord George sighed. 'I shall do all I can to recover your property, dearest. Tell me again what he has of yours, please.'

'There are at least ten letters, a silk kerchief with my initials—and a brooch Markham gave me. He would never forgive me for losing it, but the pin was loose and—*he* promised to have it repaired.'

'I dare say Blake may have sold it if it was valuable.'

'It was a diamond star and an heirloom. I was such a fool to trust him—but he was so charming and I was very unhappy.'

'You were taken in and Markham had broken your heart. I do not blame you, Verity, but we must face facts. If I am unable to conceal this business, some of the truth may come out—and if it does you would do well to throw yourself on your husband's mercy and ask him to forgive you.'

'I cannot. I would rather die.'

Lord George turned away with a sigh. It seemed he had no choice but to search Blake's house. If he were lucky enough to discover his sister's letters, he might save her from the threat of blackmail, but he had an uneasy feeling. Blake was ruthless. If he did not get what he wanted, he would find some other way of taking revenge.

The only way to free his sister of the threat was to see Blake behind bars—and that meant confessing his own guilt in the abduction of Lady Fanshawe.

It was as well that he had been prevented from saying more to Jane by the arrival of Lady Mary that morning. George had been too busy to consider marriage since his return from the army and now was not the time. He could yet be arrested and tried for the abduction of two young women.

Even had he been certain that Jane Lanchester was the woman he wished to make his wife, he could not have spoken. Besides, he wanted to be absolutely certain of his own feelings for Jane. George had seen his sister marry for the wrong reasons and some of his friends had put money and property before true affection.

Still, he believed that Jane was a brave, independent lady and the kind of woman he had looked for all his life. Given the time and opportunity he would like to know her better—but for the moment he had other things to do.

Chapter Six

'I am pleased to meet you,' Jane said as she was introduced to Lady Markham. 'Thank you for inviting us this evening. It was most kind of you.'

'Oh, that was my brother George's idea,' the lady said and then blushed. 'Forgive me, I did not mean to sound ungracious. Of course I wished to meet you. George has told me a great deal about…well, you know…'

'I dare say you have things on your mind,' Jane replied and touched her hand. 'You must not feel uncomfortable. Nothing your brother has told me will pass my lips. You have my promise.'

'Thank you. This is most awkward—forgive me, my husband is looking this way. I must enquire what he wants.'

Glancing towards her host, Jane saw a man in

his middle years. He was good-looking, but a little overweight and looked to be of a hasty temper. She saw what she thought was a sharp exchange between husband and wife and then everyone was asked to remove into the dining room.

'May I take you in, Miss Lanchester?'

Jane took Lord George's arm and smiled at him. 'You really should not have pressed your sister to invite us, sir. I think you have thrown out her arrangements.'

'I needed an excuse to see you,' he replied and laughed softly. The sound was attractive and Jane reflected that there had not been much occasion for laughter so far in their relationship. 'I shall be leaving town for a short time—on the business that you know of. I felt it only polite to tell you.'

Jane nodded. His manner was polite, but there was nothing intimate about it, but then, they had not known each other long. Circumstance had thrown them together, but he was a very distinguished and well-liked man. There was no reason he should pay her particular attention. No doubt he could have his pick of the young ladies looking for marriage.

'I have written to my brother. He should be here in a few days, sir.'

'I shall be happy to speak to Lord Lanchester when I return.'

'Your trip out of town...' she lowered her voice '...you go in search of Captain Blake?'

'I have learned of a house he owns that I did not know existed. I intend to see if he is in hiding there—and perhaps I will be able to recover Verity's property.'

'Yes, I understand. I wish you good fortune— please take care, sir. I should not like you to come to harm.'

'Thank you, Miss Lanchester. It is good of you to take an interest in my welfare after the way I behaved.'

His lips smiled, but his eyes did not reflect warmth. She wondered at his thoughts. Why did she feel that he was holding back from her? She had revealed so much of herself to him when they were fleeing from Blake, but it was almost as if they were strangers. Why had he created this barrier between them?

'I think you were a little too reckless at the

start, perhaps, but in every other way you are blameless.'

'Thank you. You are generous, Miss Lanchester.'

Still so formal and no true smile. Had she offended him? Was he trying to show her that she had no claim on him? Glancing away, she felt her cheeks become heated. She would never dream of making a claim on him—certainly none that would require a sacrifice of him. He had kissed her in a way that had seemed to indicate feeling or need, but nothing else had occurred. Did he think she would expect an offer from him?

The thought embarrassed her. Jane would never make a marriage of convenience. For her true affection and respect were all-important.

They had reached the dining room. Jane discovered she had been placed between her host and a lady she knew only slightly. Lord George held a chair for her and then took his place at the opposite side of the table. She saw the quick glance of annoyance he sent his sister's way and guessed that he had hoped to sit next to her. Since it would have been impossible to continue their conversation at the table, Jane was not too distressed at finding herself with strangers. She made pleasant conversation with her companions, noticing the odd glances her host sent his wife's way throughout the evening.

Turning to him, she said, 'It was kind of Lady Markham to invite us this evening, sir. I believe she must have had to make new arrangements for our sake?'

'My wife is fond of her brother. He asked if she would invite you, Miss Lanchester. I must say it is unlike him to make such a request. He has shown no preference for any lady of our acquaintance before this. My wife was pleased to oblige him. We should all be pleased to see him settled.'

'I hardly know Lord George,' Jane said, blushing faintly. Goodness! Was George thinking it his duty to offer? 'You must not read too much into a simple request, sir.'

'Well, I know nothing of these things, Miss Lanchester. As I said, my wife is very fond of her brother. I would she were as fond of her husband.'

Jane did not know how to reply to his very odd remark and merely smiled. Clearly, Lord

Markham had something on his mind or he would not have said such a revealing thing to a stranger. She doubted he even realised what he had said, but was merely voicing his thoughts aloud.

Did he suspect his wife of having had an affair? Could he possibly know the whole story? She certainly thought she caught a jealous look in his eye once or twice, but kept her thoughts neatly tucked away at the back of her mind. She must say nothing that would arouse suspicion, and yet something in his manner made her suspect that Lord Markham was in love with his wife and might have come to her rescue had she been brave enough to confide in him.

It was not Jane's affair to speculate on intimate matters such as these. She must not interfere. What she had been told was in the strictest confidence.

After dinner, Jane and Lady Mary took their leave of their hostess. She was able to say farewell to Lord George, but no more, for they could not linger.

* * *

George watched Jane Lanchester leave his sister's house and felt a deep regret. He cursed the moment of recklessness that had made him agree to help Blake. Had he met Jane under other circumstances, they might have stood a chance, but he could not think that she would have the slightest interest in a man who had abducted both her and one of her friends. The wonder was that she had not immediately denounced him as a rogue to his friends.

'Is something the matter, Marlowe?'

George turned his head as his brother-in-law approached him, bringing his thoughts sharply back to the present. 'No, nothing at all—I was just lost in thought.'

Lord Markham inclined his head. 'Miss Lanchester is a charming young woman. You might do much worse if you were thinking of settling down.'

'I think I could do no better,' George said with a rueful smile. 'However, I do not believe she will have me.'

'She would be a fool to turn you down, George.

You are one of the best catches on the market, dear fellow—and a good sort. Verity is very fond of you.'

'As I am of her,' George replied. Something in his brother-in-law's tone made him wonder if Verity might receive more understanding from her husband than she believed. 'Are you bothered about something yourself?'

'No...' Lord Markham hesitated. 'Nothing at all.'

George looked at him thoughtfully. Markham was hiding his thoughts, as he himself had earlier. It was a pity that Verity would not make a clean breast of things to her husband. He was fairly sure that it would clear the air between them so that they could begin again—but, since she was not prepared to take the chance, George must try once again to recover her property.

'Well, I have an early start, so I shall take my leave of you, Markham.'

'Going out of town again?'

'Yes. Business takes me away for a few days. Excuse me, I must say goodnight to Verity.'

Walking away, George put his thoughts of private happiness behind him. He needed to find those damned letters—and then he was determined to bring Blake to justice, whatever the cost to himself.

'Andrew—you've arrived,' Jane said as she entered the house after a shopping trip two days later. 'I hardly expected you so soon.'

'Did you expect me?' Andrew frowned. 'I received some interesting information and posted up to town immediately.'

'Then you will not have had my letter?'

'You wrote to me—about?'

'Lord Lanchester,' Lady Mary said, turning to greet him and interrupting their conversation. 'How lovely to see you again so soon. I do hope you have come to stay for a while this time?'

'I could remove to a hotel if it is inconvenient, ma'am. I had business here—and wished to consult Jane on a matter of some importance.'

'Naturally, you will stay here,' Lady Mary said. 'I should not dream of your going to a hotel. You are very welcome whenever you choose to visit.'

'Thank you.' He reached out and took her hand

to kiss it. 'It is a while since I visited London for pleasure. Perhaps I may accompany you this evening?'

'We go to a ball,' Lady Mary said. 'Lady Mellors is a good friend and will not mind my bringing an extra gentleman guest in the least. The more gentlemen the better.'

'Then I shall be pleased to escort you.' Andrew bowed his head and then glanced at Jane. 'When you have a moment to spare, I should be grateful if we could have a quiet word?'

'Of course. I shall just go up and tidy myself—and then we shall talk.'

Jane frowned as she ran up the stairs. What had brought Andrew to town in such haste?

She was not kept long in ignorance. Andrew was waiting for her when she returned to the small back parlour. He had been standing with his hands behind his back as he gazed out into the gardens, but turned immediately to face her.

'I believe I may know the true identity of that George fellow,' he told her. 'I spoke to some of my colleagues in the regiment before I came here and one of them mentioned a name. I thought that night that I might have seen the man before, but was not sure—now I think I recall him. He was an officer in another regiment, but his sister was rumoured to be involved with a Captain Blake…'

'Yes, I know,' Jane said, her cheeks taking fire as he stared at her. 'The man I knew as simply George is actually Lord George Marlowe—and, well, I cannot tell you the rest for it was told to me in confidence. I shall tell you that I believe him to be a man of honour despite what happened.'

'When did you discover this?' Andrew frowned. 'Was that the reason for your letter?'

'What I may tell you is that Lord George became involved in the whole sordid affair in order to recover some property from Blake. I believe him when he says that he was told it was merely an elopement—and I know that he is truly sorry for his part in the affair.'

'That is as may be.' Andrew's mouth thinned. 'If you know all this, perhaps you can tell me where I can find this…gentleman?'

'I believe he is out of town,' Jane replied. 'He

has discovered something, a house he did not know of previously, and intends to make a search for his property—and Blake.'

'I wish he had waited for me. From what I have learned of this Captain Blake, he is a ruthless devil. Lord George might be killed...' He broke off as Jane gasped. 'I hope you have not become attached to the fellow, Jane. You should not place too much trust in what he tells you. He may yet be a scoundrel and a rogue for all we know.'

'You are too harsh, Andrew. Had Lord George been a rogue, he would not have rescued either Mariah or me. I believe he has risked a great deal to do so.'

'You may be right. However, Blake must be brought to justice. He has been thwarted once, but a man like that will not rest until he has what he needs—and that is a great deal of money. One of the things I discovered from my colleagues in the regiment is that he is deeply in debt. As I understand it, his family estate in Devon is to be sold by the bank soon.'

'Then he may try again.' Jane looked at him anxiously. 'Will Mariah be safe?'

'Mariah and her friends are going abroad as soon as it can be arranged,' Andrew said. 'She is almost well enough to think of a sea journey. In the meantime, she does not leave the house alone. Avonlea has doubled the patrols about his estate and the men have been told to challenge strangers and shoot if necessary.'

'I am glad to hear it. I do not think she could bear to have such a thing happen again.'

'Mariah is of a stronger constitution than you might think, though still very quiet and reserved, most unlike herself. It is touching to see her so affected. Perhaps that is why I feel so angry with a man who ought to have known better than to become embroiled in such an affair.'

'You have seen her recently?'

'I visited before I left for London. I was sure you would be anxious for news of her.'

'Yes, I am glad to know she is recovering,' Jane said. 'Being abducted *is* alarming, though I was fortunate.'

'Mariah was drugged for a lot of the time. Lucinda confided to me that Mariah has told her a little more of her ordeal. Apparently, she screamed and fought her captors so violently that Blake forced her to drink something to keep her quiet. You were more fortunate, Jane.'

'Yes, indeed, for I had help. Mariah's fate might well have been mine had Lord George not been there to help me.'

Andrew fixed her with a hard stare. 'I must repeat my warning, Jane. I will not consider any type of a relationship between you and Lord George.'

'Yes, I see that,' Jane said quietly. She lifted her head, keeping the pain his words had caused hidden. 'Excuse me, I must go and change. We have an appointment this afternoon.'

Jane's head was high as she left the parlour, but inside she was weeping. Andrew thought he was in the right but he could not know that her heart was already engaged.

Blake's Devonshire house was in darkness when George reached it. It appeared empty and, from various signs of neglect in the grounds, he guessed that it must have been closed for some months. He could not know if Blake kept a caretaker in residence, but, after checking both the front, back and sides of what was a modest country estate, he believed there was no one in the property.

Until Verity had told him of Blake's love nest, he had not known of its existence and he had great hopes of finding his sister's letters before the night was through.

His search had told him that no windows or doors had been left carelessly open. The only way he could gain entrance was by breaking a window. He would be breaking the law, a serious offence, which could carry a prison sentence if he were caught. However, he had no choice for he could see no other way of discovering his sister's letters.

He took a pistol from his pocket and gave a pane of glass a sharp tap. Pushing the window through with a gloved fist, he found the catch and opened it. The space was just large enough for him to squeeze through.

Looking about him, he discovered that he was in a small parlour, which was still furnished with pretty items that might please a lady. The idea that Blake had brought other young women here, perhaps to seduce and blackmail them, brought a bitter taste to his mouth. He must have been mad to have had anything to do with the villain—and Verity must wish she had never met him.

The thought of his sister's anguish spurred him on and he lit a candle with the tinderbox he carried in his pocket. It was a risk because the light would show in the windows and might warn a caretaker who lived in a cottage nearby or even Blake if he were in hiding here.

Where would Blake be likely to hide letters and personal items? George approached a small desk standing near the window. It had one long drawer at the top and three down either side, its writing surface covered in green leather. He opened the top drawer and found several papers, all of which appeared to be unpaid bills, some of them recent. His pulses quickened, because it was clear that Blake had been here recently. A search of the other drawers revealed more bills. It was obvious why Blake had resorted to villainy. He must be quite desperate. If he dared to show his face in London, he would probably be arrested for debt and sent to prison.

Desperate men were dangerous. George knew he must work quickly. He went from room to room, searching chests of drawers, sideboards, desks and anything that looked as if it might conceal papers or intimate items. He was quick, but thorough. By the time he reached the library he was beginning to wonder if the letters still existed. Blake had certainly not been careless with them.

The library had shelves on every wall, which were filled with leather-bound books—books that looked as if they had never been read. To move and open all the books would take hours. He did not have that much time. Every minute he spent here the danger that someone might come grew stronger. It was sacrilege, but George knew he had no choice. He moved along the shelves pulling all the books down, several at a time, and letting them fall to the floor.

Many of them opened, but no letters fell out from between the pages. It looked as if he might go away empty handed. There was but one shelf left to empty. He took hold of a book and knew immediately it was different—not a row of books at all, but a container meant to look like five books. In fact, it was a box and by the feel of it there were several items inside. George sought and found the catch. Inside were three bundles of letters, a silk scarf and a kerchief with his sister's initials. A further search did not reveal the brooch Blake had promised to have mended for Verity.

At least he had the letters. George thrust them inside his coat. He was wondering whether he should stop to replace the books when he heard a noise. Someone was in the house! Either the caretaker had come to investigate or Blake had arrived. There was no time to repair the damage he had done in the library. He must leave immediately.

George blew out the candle and went to the long windows that let so much light into the large room. He unfastened the catch and scrambled through just as someone entered the library through the door.

'What the devil! Damnation…come back, you rogue!'

George recognised Blake's voice even as he jumped to the ground and started to run. Moments later, Blake appeared in the window and a shot was fired. The ball passed through George's coat, scraping his left shoulder, but not piercing the flesh. He ignored the stinging sensation and ran towards the sheltered spot where he had tethered his horse.

Blake fired again but George was now far enough away for the shot to fall short. He was breathing hard, the adrenalin pumping when he mounted and rode away. Luck had been with him. He had Verity's letters and her kerchief. The brooch was missing, but she could surely come up with some excuse for its loss.

George's heart was thudding in his chest as his horse responded to his urgency and they raced away, yet he had a sense of elation. Verity was safe. Now at last, he could do the right thing and go to the magistrates to lay a charge of kidnap and assault against Blake.

'I can never thank you enough,' Verity said as she pounced on her letters and the kerchief. 'They are all here, everything except the brooch.'

'It was not with the other things,' George said. 'I searched the whole house, Verity. It is my opinion that the rogue sold it.'

'Yes, perhaps.' She looked doubtful. 'It was something I was quite fond of. Markham gave it to me when we were first wed. However, you have done more than I could have expected.' She took hold of his arm to give him a hug, bringing a wince of pain from his lips. 'What is wrong— have you hurt your arm?'

'Blake returned as I was searching the library. I had left it until the last and he was in the house before I realised. I escaped through the window, but he got off a shot that just winged me. It is but a scratch, Verity, though a little sore.'

'Forgive me.' Tears stung her eyes. 'You have saved my marriage—and me from ruin. I am so grateful, dearest George. Your poor arm—it is all my fault.'

'I am glad to have brought the matter to a close as far as you are concerned,' George said and smiled at her, feeling warm affection. 'Now I must do something I should have done sooner.'

Verity looked up at him. 'You will not go to

a magistrate? No, George, think of the scandal. They will want to know why you agreed—and all your trouble will be for nothing.'

'It will be my disgrace, not yours. You must disown me if need be. I have to do this, Verity. The man is a scoundrel. Yours were not the only letters I found—there were some belonging to another married lady. I happen to know her address and I have returned them to her. If Blake is not stopped, he will continue his evil work. Other women will be blackmailed and another innocent girl may be abducted.'

'But you will be ruined if you confess your part in the affair.'

'It is a chance I must take. There are mitigating circumstances. I must hope that Lord Lanchester will testify to my rescuing his sister and Lady Fanshawe. Besides, honour demands that I take my punishment.'

'Please do not risk everything for the sake of honour, George.'

'I must do this,' he replied, his mouth set hard. His manner at that moment was arrogant and proud. 'It is important to me. I have to redeem myself in Miss Lanchester's eyes. I know there is no chance of a relationship between us—but I want her to think well of me.'

'She means so much to you?'

'Yes, she does.'

Verity's eyes misted with tears. 'In saving me you have ruined your own life. Forgive me.'

'There is nothing to forgive,' George said and touched her hand. 'You mean a great deal to me, Verity. I made a mistake in trusting Blake's word. In my arrogance I thought I could rescue the lady with none the wiser, but I was wrong. I can only hope that when my trial comes that will be taken into consideration.'

'I am sure Miss Lanchester would not wish you to make such a sacrifice just to gain her good opinion.'

'Nothing you can say will change my mind.' George bent his head to kiss her on the cheek. 'Be happy, Verity. Forgive Markham for his lapse and make it up with him for your own sake. I believe he cares for you.'

'Perhaps.' Verity's face was pale as she gazed

up at him. 'I shall never forget what you did for me.'

'Do not blame yourself. What I do I do for my own satisfaction—because I could not live with myself if I hid the truth.'

Jane was sitting in the front parlour alone the next morning. It was early and Lady Mary had not yet risen from her bed when the visitor was announced. She rose to her feet. She felt oddly nervous, for she hardly knew Lady Markham and would not have expected a visit this early in the morning.

'Miss Lanchester, forgive me,' Lady Markham said as she entered and put up the heavy veiling that covered her pretty face. It was obvious that she had been crying. 'I had to come to you. I do not know what else to do.'

'Something is wrong—your husband?'

'Markham knows nothing yet. George found my letters for me and restored them to me. That despicable rogue fired at him and he was slightly wounded in the shoulder...'

'Lord George is hurt?' Jane was immediately alarmed. 'What can I do to help?'

'He says it is nothing but a scratch,' Lady Markham said. 'It is not his wound that worries me. He went to a magistrate and told them the whole—oh, not about my letters. He promised to keep my name out of it, but the abduction of Lady Fanshawe and your own person—and his part in it.'

'No! That was so unnecessary,' Jane cried and sat down as her legs seemed to go from under her. 'Mariah is recovering well and you have your letters—why would he do such a thing?'

'For the sake of his honour as a gentleman— and your good opinion, Miss Lanchester.'

'The foolish man…' Jane's throat closed. Would he do so much for her? 'He should not have…for my sake. It is too much. Do you know what has happened?'

'He was able to send me a note, asking me to employ a lawyer for him. He is in Newgate prison, though not in the common rooms. George took some money with him when he made his confession and he has paid for easement.'

'We must be grateful for that,' Jane replied. 'Have you contacted his lawyer?'

'I stopped on my way here and handed in a letter, but I can do no more. If my husband learns of this…' She shook her head. 'I am not certain what he would say—or think. George told me that your brother might speak for him. When do you expect him?'

'He is in town at the moment,' Jane said. 'I believe he went in search of Lord George this morning. He meant to visit some of the clubs and discover his lodgings.'

'Will you speak to him? My brother has ruined himself for me and I cannot forgive myself for asking him to help me.'

'I am sure that it is no such thing. Lord George did what he thought right. Please do not distress yourself. I shall speak to my brother as soon as he returns.'

'Then I must leave you, for I was meant to go down to the country with my husband today. How can I leave London when George is in trouble?'

'You should behave as normal,' Jane said and

stood up as the shock receded and her head cleared. 'Perhaps this can be settled without too much scandal. Leave it to me, Lady Markham. I shall do what I can to help your brother. I owe him my life. I shall remind my brother of that when he returns and beg him to help Lord George.'

'Thank you so much.' Lady Markham was clearly relieved. 'If you will help him, I can leave with a clear conscience.'

Jane assured her she would do all she could and the lady went away. Pacing the floor, Jane decided that she would visit Lord George at the prison before speaking to her brother. Andrew was likely to be gone for most of the day and Jane would not rest if she did nothing but sit at home. Besides, it would be best if she knew the whole rather than giving Andrew half the story.

Chapter Seven

Jane had chosen a plain dress and donned a dark cloak with a hood. Passing a fruit seller on her way to the notorious prison, she had purchased some oranges; she had also brought bread and a meat pie from the kitchens at Lady Mary's house. Lord George would soon run through the money he'd carried in his pockets if he had to pay for food to be brought in, and though his lawyer could supply him with more, she felt some relief in being able to bring him some comforts.

Outside the prison she paused, glancing up at its forbidding walls and the stout gate. Had Lord George been imprisoned for debt it would not have been quite so bad, for she knew that debtors were treated quite well and their families were able to visit every day, some choosing to live there with the prisoner, free to come and go as they pleased. Newgate was rather different to the Fleet.

She rang the bell outside. A small opening appeared at the top of the gate as a panel slid across and a face peered out at her.

'State yer business, miss.'

'I have come to visit one of the prisoners,' Jane said, raising her head proudly. 'Lord George Marlowe. He was brought here yesterday, to await trial, I believe.'

'Yeah, he be here. I suppose yer can come in fer a short visit. What have yer got in the basket?'

'Food,' Jane said and offered the basket, hiding her feelings as he rifled the through the food with his grimy hands and took an orange. She slipped her hand in her pocket and took out a shilling, holding it out to him. 'For your trouble, sir.'

He nodded, took the coin and bit it, then slipped it into his coat pocket. 'I'll take yer to him, but yer can only stay fer ten minutes.'

'Thank you. You are most kind.'

Jane followed through the courtyard. There were various buildings on both sides and some men and women were walking in the yard. They all looked slightly dirty and unkempt, and she realised these must be favoured inmates who had been allowed to come out for some air. Three of the men were wearing irons on their legs.

Pray God that Lord George had not been subjected to such barbarous treatment!

Jane's throat tightened as they went into the main building. The air inside was fetid and she had to hold her breath for a moment to keep herself from feeling sick. What a terrible place this was! She was distressed that George should have been brought to this merely through a need to clear himself in her eyes. The foolish man. There had been no need to do such a thing for her sake.

She had not been mistaken in him. He was as honourable, kind and generous as she had thought him when they were escaping.

The gaoler led her past rows of cells where prisoners were herded together, both men and women, all in large cells without a stick of furniture between them. A shudder went through her as she wondered how they slept or ate—or performed any other bodily function. The smell was quite appalling.

As he led her up some stairs to what seemed a better part of the prison, the air cleared a little and Jane was able to breathe more easily. She was relieved that Lord George was not being kept in the pens downstairs. No farmer worth his salt would keep animals in such conditions. It was wicked, wicked! Jane's eyes stung with tears she must not allow to fall.

When the gaoler stopped outside a wooden door with a grille in the top her pulses raced. He took a key from a large ring at his waist and opened the door.

'Ten minutes. I'll be waiting out here—no funny business.'

'Thank you.' Jane's face flamed as she saw the leer on his mouth. Did he imagine she was Lord George's mistress? Was he warning her that she must not lie with her lover? It would not be surprising that what she was doing would be thought scandalous by most of the ladies she knew. 'You are most generous, sir.'

Lord George was standing with his back towards her as she entered, but turned with an exclamation of shock as he saw her.

'Jane! Miss Lanchester—are you mad? You should not be here. You must leave at once.'

'I have only ten minutes. Forgive me, I had to come when I learned you were here, sir. Why did you do such a foolish thing? I should never have demanded such a sacrifice of you. You must have known that?'

'Would you not?' He smiled ruefully. 'I found that I could not live with myself, Miss Lanchester. I was in large part at fault for what happened to you—and to Lady Fanshawe. Besides, Blake must be brought to justice or others may suffer. I have made a clean breast of the whole and will hope to be acquitted of evil intent.'

'Yes, I agree that Blake must be caught and punished—but could you not have brought a case against him without involving yourself?'

'If he is taken, he will name me—and he will try to bring me down to his level. I hoped that I might be listened to with some sympathy, but, as you see, I am here.'

Jane placed her basket on the table and moved

towards him. 'I have brought some food. Is there anything more I can do for you? Have you received a visit from your lawyer?'

'Not yet, but it is early days. If you wish, you could ask Verity for some clean clothes. I forgot that when I wrote to her.'

'Verity is leaving town with her husband. I should be happy to bring them to you, if you will give me the direction of your town house so that I may fetch them.'

'You should not think of coming here again, Miss Lanchester.'

'I could give them to your lawyer.'

'Well...' He hesitated, then, 'I will furnish you with the address on one condition—you ask your brother to bring the clothes. You must not risk yourself further for my sake, Miss Lanchester.'

'Very well, if that is your wish. Will you not call me Jane once more, Lord George? I had thought us friends of sorts after what we've been through. I wish to be your friend still if you will allow it.'

His eyes went over her. 'Had we met in other circumstances, I should have wished for more,

Jane—but I fear it is too late to hope for anything. Your brother would not tolerate such a thing and nor should he. I am ruined and I would not drag you down with me.'

'I am old enough to make my own choices,' Jane said, a stubborn note in her voice. 'Please do not despair, my lord. I shall talk to Andrew. I am certain he will speak for you. We shall get you out of this dreadful place somehow.'

'Thank you.' George hesitated, then moved towards her, reaching for her hand. 'I wanted to tell you that I admire you more than any woman I have ever met...'

She moved towards him, gazing up into his face. The feeling was very strong between them and Jane's mouth opened slightly as she anticipated his kiss. She longed for him to hold her and thought for a moment he would do so, but then he gave a muffled oath as the door of the cell opened and the gaoler beckoned to her.

'You had best leave now, miss.'

'Yes, I must go.' Jane glanced at George. 'Will you allow me to visit you again?'

'It is not fitting for a girl of your good name

and character. If it were known, you would be ruined. I have no wish to bring you down as well as myself, Jane.'

She inclined her head, accepting his decision. 'God bless and care for you, sir,' she said, her throat tight. 'I shall speak to my brother. I pray that we shall meet again in happier circumstances.'

'Goodbye, Jane. I count it an honour to have known you.'

She lifted her head, following the gaoler into the narrow passageway, her eyes stinging with the tears she refused to shed as the door was locked after her.

He was such a stubborn, proud fool and she loved him so much—but this might be the last time they met. If no one spoke for him, he could be tried and condemned to the gallows.

'You did what?' Andrew's fury showed in his hard mouth and the glint in his eyes. 'Jane, how could you be such a fool? If anyone saw you go to that place, your reputation will be ruined...'

'Please do not scold me,' she said, her head

high. 'I did what I considered right. Lord George saved my life—and he rescued Mariah. Had he not done so, she might still be a prisoner and I could have been dead. Are you not in the least grateful for your sister's life?'

Andrew stared at her in silence, then his frown relaxed and he inclined his head. 'Of course I am grateful for what he did for you and for Mariah. He should have waited for me to go to the magistrate with him. I would have spoken for him.'

'His honour prevented him from relying on you. He hoped that what he had done would be seen sympathetically, but instead he was imprisoned.'

'He must have known it could happen?'

'He thought to redeem himself in my eyes.'

Andrew was silent, then, 'What is there between you?'

'Nothing but gratitude,' Jane said, crossing her fingers as she lied. 'I know that what he did in helping with the abduction was foolish and wrong—but perhaps it was meant to be. Had the circumstances been other than they were, I do not think I should be standing here now, Andrew.'

'I should be very sorry for that,' Andrew said and sighed. 'Very well, I shall do what I can. The clothes and money are easy enough, but you need influence to have someone released from Newgate. I shall speak for him at his trial but I do not think I can prevent it.'

'Is there no one who would help us?'

Andrew met her troubled gaze. 'I met Avonlea in town this morning. He has brought Lucinda up for a few days to buy some clothes she needs before it becomes difficult for her to travel. Avonlea has considerable influence. If he were persuaded that Marlowe was innocent in intent and had redeemed himself, he might be able to do the thing.'

'Will you speak to him, Andrew, or shall I?'

'He wanted to speak to you. I asked him to call this evening at six. You may put your plea to him then, Jane. I cannot be sure what he will say, but it is all we can do.'

'Thank you.' Jane's smile lit her face. 'I should be very distressed if Lord George went to the gallows, Andrew. I shall tell the duke my story and hope that he decides to take an interest.'

* * *

George looked up as he heard the key turn in the lock the following morning. He hoped the gaoler would bring him some decent food this time instead of the slop he had been given earlier. The food Jane had brought had sustained him thus far, but it had all gone and the thought of prison food made his stomach turn queasy. He was surprised as he saw the tall gentleman enter. Avonlea was not unknown to him, though they did not often mix in the same circles.

'Your Grace.' George inclined his head. 'I am sorry I can offer you no refreshment worthy of the name. To what do I owe the pleasure of this visit?'

'The eloquence of Miss Jane Lanchester,' Avonlea replied grimly. 'Her brother added a restrained plea on your behalf, Marlowe—but it was she who swayed me.'

'Miss Lanchester would do better to deny all knowledge of me.'

'I doubt she would ever do that, sir.' The duke smiled. 'She is a redoubtable lady and will make an excellent wife for someone, though she is fiercely independent. She is a little outspoken at times, but a good friend. First, I must ask you for your side of this story in your own words—and after that I have a few questions for you myself.'

'At the start, I was told the business was an elopement, but the lady wanted a little excitement so it was to appear to be an abduction.' George held up his hand in apology. 'It was a foolish mistake. I should have known that a rogue like Blake was up to no good. When I realised I had been duped I made up my mind to rescue Lady Fanshawe—but then Miss Lanchester was also taken captive and it seemed prudent to rescue her first, because I believed Lady Fanshawe to be relatively safe. Besides, Miss Lanchester began her own escape and I could not leave her to hobble about the countryside alone.'

'Why did you agree in the first place—was it matter of money?'

'No. Blake had letters and items that did not belong to him. He could have ruined someone I care for and I was blackmailed in my turn.'

'So why did you take your story to the magistrate?'

'I recovered Lady Fanshawe and the letters before doing so.' George rubbed at his shoulder, which was still a little sore. 'Blake returned to his house as I was searching it and winged me as I escaped. I dare say he will have realised who was responsible for ransacking his house—so the game was up. I thought I had no choice but to put my case and take the consequences. Besides, the sorry business sat ill with my honour as a gentleman. I acted in the way I thought best at the time, but it was reckless and foolish.'

'Yes, I see. I understand more of your feelings than you might imagine. When someone close to one is in danger or threatened, a man may do many things he would not otherwise do.' Avonlea looked at him for a moment longer. 'I must speak with some friends about your case. To my belief you have been wrongly imprisoned, sir. You went along with this business with the clear intention of protecting the lady in question. Had you not done so the abduction would still have taken place and the rogue would have got clean away. If my word counts for anything, the case against you will be dismissed. We need your help in the continuing search for Blake.'

'I give you my word that I shall leave no stone unturned in the effort to bring him to justice.'

'I imagine he will come looking for you,' the duke said, giving him a meaningful look. 'If I get you clear, you will return to society and be seen everywhere. If anyone has got wind of this business, you will say it was all a mistake—just that, nothing more. I am asking you to become a target, Marlowe. I believe it is the only way we may trap Blake, for he is a clever devil. It is my hope that he will try to take revenge for what you have done. You will be watched and we shall do all within our power to protect you, but you could lose your life. The choice is, of course, yours.'

'It is my fervent wish to do all I can to redeem myself.'

'This plan to draw Blake out is a long shot,' Avonlea said. 'He may stay clear of London—unless we can think of a way to smoke him out of his lair.'

'I could pay another visit to his house. Make certain he knows who his enemy is.'

'Yes, perhaps—but you should not go alone. I shall speak to Lord Lanchester. If we can get Blake to show his hand, we may get him sooner rather than later.'

'The sooner the better. No woman is truly safe while that devil walks the streets.'

Jane was sitting with her godmother and Andrew in the drawing room that evening when the butler announced that they had a visitor. Something made her heart catch and she gasped as Lord George walked in, looking as if he had spent the last few days buying a new wardrobe rather than languishing in prison. His blue superfine coat moulded to his shoulders in a superb fit, making her think that she had not met anyone with quite the physique of her saviour.

'You will forgive this call,' Lord George said, his eyes seeking Jane's briefly. 'I have been detained or I would have called sooner. Ladies, your servant—but it was Lord Lanchester I wished to see alone.'

'Of course. We shall not stand on ceremony. Pray take Lord George into the back parlour,

Andrew,' Lady Mary said. 'Before you go, sir, we intend to visit the theatre tomorrow evening— would you care to be part of the party?'

'I should like it very much another time,' George replied and once again his eyes went to Jane. 'However, I may need to go out of town.'

'Again?' Lady Mary's eyebrows arched. 'You are a busy man, sir. You are forever coming and going.'

'It is my hope that after this trip I shall be settled in town for a while.'

He bowed to her, glanced at Jane once more and turned to Andrew. 'If we could speak, sir?'

'Of course.' Andrew directed a frown at his sister. 'I have not forgotten that we are going out later. Please excuse me for the moment.'

'Dinner will be no more than twenty minutes.' Lady Mary glanced at Lord George. 'Can I persuade you to stay?'

'I have no wish to presume on your good nature, ma'am.'

'If you have no prior engagement, I insist.'

'Very well.' George smiled, his gaze once more resting on Jane. 'I should be delighted.'

Jane's cheeks were a little pink as she inclined her head, then glanced at her brother.

'I think I shall go upstairs for a moment,' she announced when the gentlemen had left the room. 'Please excuse me, Godmother.'

'Yes, of course, dearest.' Lady Mary smiled. 'Isn't this agreeable? Lord George is such a pleasant young man—do you not think so?'

Lord George left in Andrew's company as soon as dinner was over. Andrew apologised to his sister and Lady Mary.

'Forgive me, but I must cry off this evening, ladies. I find that I have business that will not wait. You must excuse me. I may be gone for a day or so.'

'Now that is too bad,' Lady Mary said. 'We had quite settled it that you were to stay for a few days.'

'I am certain Andrew's business is important,' Jane said. She had not missed the glance that passed between her brother and Lord George. 'I wish you a safe journey, Brother—and you also, sir.' Her eyes moved to Lord George as he came to take his leave of her. Her heart raced as their eyes met. In that moment she wished they were alone so that she could speak to him privately, but with Andrew's stern gaze on her there was little to be said. 'Take care,' she whispered as he lifted her hand to his lips.

'We shall be back before you know it,' Andrew said, unconsciously confirming her suspicions. 'No need to worry, Jane. Everything is under control.'

Lady Mary's eyes widened and she gave her goddaughter a hard stare as the two gentlemen went out.

'Now what are they up to, Jane? If you know something I do not, pray enlighten me.'

Jane hesitated. Her brother had not told Lady Mary about the abductions or the shooting in their garden or the fact that Jane's life might still be in danger. Clearly she needed to set her god-mother's mind at rest. She spoke carefully, for she did not wish to alarm her godmother unduly, giving only the barest details and leaving out the fact that she might still be in danger.

'I knew you were hiding something. Pray tell

me why your brother and Lord George are leaving town together?'

'I think it has something to do with the man who abducted Mariah Fanshawe and myself. Andrew is determined to bring the rogue to justice and so is Lord George.'

'I can understand you brother's involvement, but what has this affair to do with Lord George?' Lady Mary's brows shot up.

'That I cannot tell you. No, really, I cannot, dearest Godmother. You must ask him yourself if you wish for an answer.'

'I shall certainly do so when we next meet. You must know that I consider him a good match for you, Jane. His family would love to see him married—and, though you say you do not wish to wed, I fear that you will miss so much in life if you do not.'

'Yes, perhaps you are right.' Jane smiled at her, hiding the emotions that churned inside her. Her thoughts were in turmoil, for although she had quite decided not to marry, she did like Lord George so very much. If only she could be certain that he felt the same about her! 'We should get ready if we are not to be late, Godmother.'

'You are trying to change the subject, Jane.' Lady Mary wagged a finger at her. 'I shall allow you to do so—but please think about what I have said, dearest. It would give me such pleasure to see you happy.'

'I shall think about it,' Jane promised.

She could think of hardly anything else these days. Indeed, she had found the idea of marriage creeping into her mind too often of late. She was too honest a girl to hide the truth from herself. Lord George had aroused feelings that she had never imagined she would experience, feelings so strong that she was hard put to conceal them from her family.

If they had met in different circumstances, she thought that she might have been a very happy young woman. A proposal from Lord George would have brought great pleasure to both her and her family—but in the current situation Jane knew her brother would never countenance her marriage.

No, no, she must not let herself think such

thoughts. The gentleman had not given her any reason to imagine that he felt more than liking for her. Besides, everything was in such chaos. They were all still in danger while Blake was at large and marriage must be the last thing on Lord George's mind just now.

Where were her brother and Lord George going that night—and what did they intend? She prayed that it was not as dangerous as she feared.

'Please keep them both safe,' she murmured as she went to tidy herself before leaving for their evening engagement. 'I would not have either of them come to harm.'

'Your plan is to search the house again, and you wish Blake to see you—do I have that correct?'

They had been riding throughout the night and for much of the day, stopping to rest their horses when necessary. During the journey, George had explained that he wanted to confront Blake face to face if it were possible, hoping to draw his fire.

'I have not yet recovered a diamond brooch he stole from someone dear to me. I do not expect to find it and indeed I would not bother to search for something I imagine has been sold. Avonlea suggested another search in the hope of drawing Blake's fire. You will remain outside the house, Lanchester. If you hear shots, use your own judgement.'

'It may be too late by then,' Andrew replied. 'Blake will kill you if he can. Avonlea told you that I should watch your back and that is just what I shall do. No arguments, Marlowe. We are in this together. I am determined that Blake shall not escape justice. He deserves to hang for what he did to Lady Fanshawe—and my sister, though Jane has taken it in her stride, of course.'

'Miss Lanchester is a very brave and sensible woman, but her fate might have been otherwise. Had things gone badly, Blake might have murdered her and disposed of her body. I believe him to be quite ruthless.'

Andrew frowned. 'I know my obligation to you, sir. All the more reason why I should accompany you into the house. I should not forgive myself if I stood by while that rogue murdered you.'

'Very well, two of us are better than one,'

George said. 'If anything should happen to me, you will tell Jane that I have done all I could to put right the wrong I was party to?'

'I believe she already knows,' Andrew said, a thoughtful expression on his face. 'We must hope that Blake is still in residence. It is possible that he has found a new hole to hide in.'

'Someone is in the house,' George said as they saw the light in a room at the back. 'It seems foolish to waste time searching the house. If he is here, we should confront him and offer him a chance to give himself up.'

'And if he will not come quietly?'

'There are two of us. We should make him our prisoner and then let Avonlea deal with him. I dare say Lady Fanshawe will wish to testify against the rogue.'

'Lady Fanshawe knew her abductor, but Avonlea will not wish to drag her name through the courts. He intended to deal with this himself.' Andrew's mouth drew into a thin line. 'At the start I would have seen him tried for his crime— but if he tries to escape I shall shoot to kill.'

'It is always best to take the lawful course if possible,' George said. 'If I am forced to fire, I shall, but I would seek to maim rather than kill.'

'You have sympathy for the rogue?'

'None—but I prefer the law to take its course.'

'What if Blake reveals your part in the affair? It will bring scandal to your name, for it is bound to get out.'

'That is the chance I must take.'

'Very well. You must abide by your conscience, sir. I shall follow mine.'

'We are agreed.'

They shook hands, then looked towards the back of the house as a door opened and a man came out. Blake stood for a moment as if in thought and then began to walk towards where they had taken cover behind the stable.

'Damn! Where is he going?'

'Probably to find an inn and get drunk.'

'It is now or never,' George said. 'I'm going to confront him. Stay behind me unless you are needed.'

He walked out from behind the corner of the stable block, his pistol cocked and held firmly in his right hand. Blake saw him instantly, hesitated, his expression murderous.

'What the hell are you doing here?'

'I have come to bring you to justice, Blake. You tricked me into helping you abduct two innocent women. For that you deserve punishment. In my opinion, you should hang, but the judge will decide your fate.'

'And if I do not care to accompany you?'

'You have little choice, sir.'

Andrew came out from behind the stable block, also pointing a pistol in Blake's direction.

'Damn! How many more of you are there?' Blake's eyes were everywhere, his face pale. 'Who the hell are you, anyway?'

'You took my sister when you abducted Lady Fanshawe,' Andrew said. 'You made enemies that day, sir—powerful enemies—and now it is time to pay the price.'

'To hell with you!' Blake grunted, his hand going to his pocket. He fired through the cloth of his coat, narrowly missing Lord George, who stumbled against Andrew, causing him to misfire his pistol. Seizing his chance, Blake turned and plunged into the shrubbery.

Andrew swore and grabbed George's pistol, firing after the fugitive. He heard a cry and knew that he had found his target, but Blake clutched at his shoulder and kept running.

'Damn it,' Andrew muttered and began to reload his own pistol as fast as he could. 'I merely winged him.' He pointed his gun in the direction Blake had disappeared and then lowered his arm. 'Which way did he go? We must search for him.'

'We might have done better to wait until he was drunk,' George said and looked rueful. 'I am sorry for spoiling your shot, Lanchester.'

'Was it an accident?'

'His shot was too close. My reaction was to jerk aside and I stumbled into you.'

'It is a pity my aim was not true with the second shot.' Andrew's expression was grim. 'Have you any idea where he would go?'

'None…' Hearing the sound of hoofbeats, George pointed and they both swung round as Blake raced away on horseback. 'He must have found our horses. He's taken your horse, Lanchester.'

Andrew cursed and fired, but Blake was moving too fast and the shot went wide.

'Curse the rogue. Now what do we do?'

'I'll go after him. You will find horses in the stable. Take your pick and follow me. We must try to catch up to him. He will be like a wounded beast now—and more dangerous than ever.'

'Yes, do not wait for me. Go after him—and if you get the chance, shoot to kill.'

It was noon the following day when the two men met up again. They looked at each other. Andrew shook his head and George frowned.

'We missed our chance,' he said. 'Blake will not go back to his house again. He will find somewhere to hide up and lick his wounds.'

'What else will he do, that is the question that troubles me,' Andrew said grimly. 'I do not think he will allow this to go unrevenged, Marlowe. He is not the kind of man to lick his wounds for long. He will try for some kind of retaliation. He knows we are out to get him and he will make his plans accordingly.'

'We must both watch our backs,' George said. 'I am for London—what of you?'

'I shall accompany you. I must be there in a week's time anyway. There is some business that will not wait. I must make arrangements before then, because with that cobra at large I fear for my sister.'

'Jane?' George's eyes narrowed. 'You think he might try to strike at you through your sister?'

Andrew's gaze met his. 'In his shoes, what would you do?'

'We must return to London with all speed,' George said. 'Jane could be in terrible danger.'

Chapter Eight

Jane sat before the dressing mirror, watching as her godmother's maid twisted her hair up on the top of her head, arranging its glossy lengths in curls and allowing a small bunch of ringlets to cascade onto her nape.

'I think it suits you very well this way, Miss Lanchester. It is less severe than your old style, if you do not mind my saying so.'

'Thank you, Milton. It looks very well. I am ready now. Please do not feel you need wait up for me this evening.'

'It is my pleasure to attend you, miss. I should be failing in my duty if I did not.'

Jane stood. 'Very well, thank you. I shall go to my godmother now.'

She was thoughtful as she went downstairs.

They were to dine with friends of Lady Mary's this evening, and then go on to a card party later. Would her brother and Lord George have returned by the time the evening was over? She was impatient to hear from them, but subdued her anxiety as she saw her godmother talking to her housekeeper in the hall.

'Ah, there you are, dearest,' Lady Mary said. 'We must be prompt this evening, for Mrs Buxton does not like to keep her cook waiting. It is so difficult to find servants who suit one, and she does have a rather splendid cook, as you will discover when we dine.'

'You also have an excellent chef, Godmother.'

'Yes, my dear, but...' Lady Mary lowered her voice as they went out. 'My chef does not compare with Madame Felice. Her soufflés are truly to die for, my love.'

'Then we must certainly not keep our hostess waiting,' Jane said with a smile. 'I remember we once had the most dreadful cook. Poor Papa was forever complaining about his beef and Mama did not know what to do...'

* * *

The drive to Mrs Buxton's house was much taken up by talk of the difficulty in finding good servants.

Their carriage drew up outside their hostess's house. A linkboy was holding a torch aloft to light the path for the guests, who were arriving one after the other.

Jane gave her hand to the groom and stepped down. Glancing at his face, she thought that she had not seen him before. Her godmother's head groom must have employed a new man.

'Thank you,' she said and turned to look at her godmother.

The door was opened as they approached, and the butler bowed and welcomed them to the house, standing back to admit them. About to step inside, Jane glanced back and discovered that the new groom was watching her. For some reason she felt cold at the nape of her neck, but dismissed the odd little shiver as she went into the lights and warmth.

'My dear Lady Mary—and Miss Lanchester.'

Mrs Buxton came bustling towards them, her silk skirts rustling as she exuded the scent of lavender water. 'I am so delighted that you could both come this evening.'

'We were happy to accept,' Lady Mary said and kissed the proffered cheek. 'I have been telling Jane about your cook.'

'Madame Felice is beyond compare, a treasure.' The lady beamed. 'Wait until you see what she has prepared for us this evening. I think she has excelled herself.'

Jane smiled as the two ladies walked ahead of her, engrossed in their talk. Mrs Buxton was one of her godmother's very best friends and the two always had much to talk about.

The drawing room was filled with ladies and gentlemen of a similar age to Lady Mary. Jane liked her godmother's friends, but sometimes these evenings could be a little tedious. She could not help her thoughts straying now and then to Lord George. Where was he and what was he doing? Was he with her brother? Did he think of her at all?

* * *

'So, Miss Lanchester. How are you enjoying your visit to town this time?'

Jane turned her attention to the gentleman at her side. He was a man of middle years, stout and serious, but kind and with a reputation for generosity. She knew him to take a great interest in the unfortunate people of London.

'I am enjoying it very well, sir,' she replied. 'I believe you have recently founded a hospital for the poor of London, Sir James?'

'Yes, indeed that is true. I am looking for people of good character to sit on the board, Miss Lanchester. Would you be interested in becoming one of my governors?'

'That sounds very interesting, sir. It is something I should like very much were I in town permanently. However, I think Lady Mary goes to Bath soon and then I shall return home to the country.'

'A pity. I should have liked a lady of your good sense to join us—but perhaps one day, when you marry?'

'If I have occasion to spend more time in London, I should be happy to join you, sir.'

The butler had announced dinner. Sir James offered his arm, escorting her into the dining room. He was seated on her left hand and spent the next hour or more telling her about his various good works. On her right was a gentleman of advanced years, whose only comments concerned the excellence of the meal they were served.

It was some two and a half hours later when Jane and Lady Mary took their leave of Mrs Buxton. Jane thanked her hostess for a very pleasant evening and walked a little ahead of Lady Mary, who lingered to talk with her friend for a moment longer in the hall.

Jane approached the carriage, which was drawn up and waiting for them at the side of the road. The groom opened the door for her, giving her his hand to help her inside. Jane took it and climbed into the closed carriage, settling back against the squabs. To her astonishment the groom followed her inside and pulled the door shut. Even as she protested, the vehicle started off and her cry of alarm was cut short as the man drew a pistol and pointed it at her.

'It is useless to call for help, Miss Lanchester,' he said. 'You are being abducted and my orders are to shoot you if you try to escape.'

Jane caught the rope that hung from a metal ring above the door and hung on. The horses were in such a frenzy of speed that she was in danger of being flung across the carriage.

'Is your driver trying to kill us both?'

'He will drive more slowly once we are safe away. Be sensible, miss, for I do not want to harm you.'

'I am hardly likely to throw myself out,' Jane replied, for to do so would be certain injury or even death. 'Pray put the pistol away, sir. It may otherwise go off and injure one of us.'

The groom eyed her uncertainly. 'I was told to be wary of you. He said you were too clever for your own good.'

'I suppose by *he* you mean Captain Blake?'

The groom looked at her with suspicious eyes. 'I've been paid to do a job, miss. I know he is a cold cove—and dangerous to cross.'

'Yes, I imagine he is,' Jane said. 'Why has he ordered you to abduct me? I am not an heiress. He will gain little from this, I assure you.'

'I don't know what he wants from you, miss. I do what I'm told and that's the end of it.'

Jane sat back against the squabs, studying the face of the man opposite. He had not lowered his guard or put away his pistol. Clearly, he was afraid that she might try to jump from the speeding carriage, which had slowed sufficiently for her to let go of the rope, but was still too swift for her to risk throwing herself out.

'What did you intend to do had my godmother accompanied me to the carriage?'

'I was told to bring her, too, if there was no choice.'

'What happened to the coachman?'

'We jumped him as he got down to ease his thirst while you were in the house. He had a little knock on the head, but he'll be right as rain when he wakes.'

'How many of you are there?'

'Two more,' the groom replied. 'Had you been difficult I should have called for help. It's as well the old lady stopped to gossip. She might have been hurt. I do not hold with hurting ladies, miss.'

'And yet you were prepared to kidnap me?'

'No choice, miss. He says you'll come to no harm if you behave yourself.'

'That has set my mind greatly at ease,' Jane said a trifle ironically. She lapsed into silence, her mind working swiftly.

Blake had had her abducted—why? Did he hope to gain a financial reward? She was not a rich heiress like Mariah, but she supposed Andrew could raise a few thousand guineas for her ransom. Yet why had it happened now?

Jane believed there might be more than a mere ransom behind her abduction. However, there was little she could do for the moment. With a pistol aimed relentlessly at her chest, she could only wait for the opportunity to present itself. Besides, she would like to know why she had been abducted.

'Thank goodness you are both here,' Lady Mary cried as she entered the house some time later that evening and saw Andrew standing with Lord

George in the hall. 'I did not know what to do. I was never more shocked in my life. It happened right before my eyes, outside Mrs Buxton's house.'

She gave a little moan of distress and swayed. Lord George moved to support her. 'What is wrong, dear lady—and where is Jane?'

'She was abducted—right under my nose, if you please. We were leaving Mrs Buxton's house, where we had dined. I stopped to speak with our hostess at the door. Jane had said her farewells and entered the coach. Before I knew what was happening, the rascal jumped in with her and the coach set off at such a pace. I was stunned. For a moment I did not know what to think and then I realised that they had stolen the coach and made off with my goddaughter.'

'Blake. Damn his soul to hell,' George said, his mouth set in a grim line. 'He must have come straight to London and taken her.'

'He would hardly have had time,' Andrew replied, a glint in his eyes. 'If you ask me, he has been planning this for a while. Whoever did this must have known where you would be this evening, Lady Mary, and had access to your stables.'

'I think there was a new groom,' Lady Mary said. 'Coachman told me he had taken on a new man to replace someone who had left without warning.' Her eyes widened in distress. 'Do you think…?'

'I think it very likely that your groom was either paid to abscond or disposed of in some way. It was the only way to infiltrate your service and get close to Jane. They must also have influenced your coachman in some way—or incapacitated him—in order to make off with your coach and Jane.'

'I do hope they have not harmed Billings. He has been with me for thirty years.' Lady Mary made a choking sound. 'Who has done this dreadful thing to Jane? Please tell me the whole truth. Jane told me about the abduction, but I thought that was all over.'

'I told you that I wanted to remove Jane from the country for a while and that she had had a little fright.' Andrew frowned. 'I should have told you everything when she was abducted. The rogue has not been caught and may be looking for revenge on both her and Lord George. It may be he that has her snatched.'

'No! Why did you not tell me all of it? Had I known, I should have been more careful of her. Had my coachman been aware of danger, this could not have happened.'

'Jane was not the intended victim the first time. The rogues who took her did so because she tried to stop them abducting someone else.'

'I must sit down,' Lady Mary said. 'We should all have some brandy. You will tell me the whole—and what you plan to do to rescue Jane.'

'This is our fault,' George said, his face white with strain. 'You will excuse me, Lady Mary. I had agents watching Jane. I must speak to them, discover what they know of this affair.'

He strode from the house, his expression grim. Lady Mary watched him go, then turned to Andrew.

'You have some serious explaining to do, sir. I wish to know who abducted my goddaughter and why she is still in danger.'

They had been travelling for no more than half an hour at most when the coach began to slow down. Jane decided that must mean that they were either still in London or on the outskirts.

'Where are we?' she asked, looking at her captor apprehensively. 'What is happening?'

'Please do not ask me any more questions, miss,' the man replied. 'He gave me orders to bring you here and that's all I know. He said nothing bad would happen if you behaved yourself.'

'You believed him?' Jane raised her head. 'I hope he paid you well, sir, for abduction is a hanging offence—and since he did not take part, you would hang while he escaped punishment.'

'We had no choice, miss. When Blake tells you to do something, you do it—if you want to live.'

'Indeed? Why do you work for such a master?'

'He ain't my master. I take his money, but no man is my master.'

'Your employer, then. Surely you must know that he is an evil man and capable of any infamy?'

'I may know it now, but I didn't when I started to work for him. He were in a rare temper when I last saw him. I believe he will be waiting for us—and if I were you I should be careful of what you say to him, miss.'

'I am quite interested in meeting Captain Blake,' Jane said. The door of the coach had been opened and another groom stood waiting to help her down. He was also armed, his face half covered with a mask. 'I am hardly likely to try to escape with two of you pointing pistols at me. Pray put them away. I have no intention of trying to escape—at least until I have spoken to your employer.'

'I've got her, Jed,' the first man grunted and pocketed his pistol before grasping Jane's arm firmly. 'She ain't going to run if she has any sense. This is a rum area in the day and at night she would soon find herself in trouble.'

The sky was quite dark with only a sprinkling of stars, but the light from the carriage lantern gave Jane an indication of her whereabouts. She glanced about her as the man propelled her towards what was clearly an inn of sorts. Its appearance was shabby from outside, the yard littered with animal droppings, bits of straw and other debris. A lantern hung above the door and the sound of water lapping against its banks told her that she was near the river. The narrow streets behind them were unlit, and the buildings shrouded in darkness. She thought some might be warehouses, for she suspected they were in what appeared to be a derelict area of the docks.

One of the grooms knocked at the inn door and it was opened, light from inside spilling out.

'That you, Stark? We thought yer were never coming,' a man grunted. 'Have yer got her?'

'I had to wait my chance,' Stark replied. 'They were a long time in the house. Is he here?'

'Aye, and he's in a rare mood.'

'I expected that…'

Jane was pushed inside a dark hall that smelled strongly of ale, smoke and stale cooking odours. The man who had opened the door squinted at her, then jerked his head.

'Bring her upstairs. He won't see her tonight. Someone shot him in the arm and he's in pain. He's been drinking for two hours, swearin' and cursin'. We'll lock her in and she can wait fer the mornin'.' He peered at Jane in the gloom. 'She ain't tied up. Be careful she don't escape like the last time.'

'It isn't necessary to tie me,' Jane said, looking at the man who had captured her. 'Please, Mr Stark, do not listen to him. You have done your work. If called upon to testify, I should say that you did no more than necessary and did not harm me. You would do very much better to let me go and save your own neck.'

'Shut yer mouth,' the innkeeper said. 'Any more of yer lip and I'll shut it fer yer.'

'No need to be rude to the young lady, Rab. She can't escape this time. Went out of the window at the last place, but there's nothing to break her fall here.'

He gave Jane a little push towards the stairs. 'Up you go, miss. I shan't tie you up. I told you, I don't hold with hurting ladies.'

Jane made no reply as she walked up the stairs, which were dark and narrow. The man ahead of them was carrying a chamberstick, which threw out just enough light for her to see her way. She knew that for the moment she must do as she was told. There were too many men about and not all of them would be as considerate as Stark if she tried to escape.

The innkeeper led the way into a small chamber furnished with a bed and little else but a battered chest of drawers. He touched his flame to a stub of candle in an iron stick standing on the chest. For a moment there was more light and Jane could see the men's faces clearly. The innkeeper was a rascally-looking creature, dirty, with a scar at his temple and a lazy eyelid that made him squint. Stark looked like a man who had been used to better things, neat and clean and close shaven—he might have been a lawyer or a clerk in a previous life.

'I'll bring you some wine,' Stark told her. 'You've had a shock and it will help you to sleep, miss. The bed is clean. Rab keeps decent rooms, even if his person leaves something to be desired.'

''Ere, you callin' me names, Stark?'

'I was reassuring Miss Lanchester that your bedding was clean. She need not fear to pick up lice here.'

'I keeps a good house,' the innkeeper muttered

and went towards the door. 'Make sure yer lock her in or he'll have somethin' ter say in the morning.'

'Try not to fret, miss,' Stark said. 'Rab won't hurt you—and the cap'n told me you would come to no harm.'

'Thank you...' Jane hesitated, then, 'You said no man was your master. I do not know what Captain Blake paid you to bring me here, but my brother will pay you more if you help me to get away. Please consider my offer, sir. I think you a good man at heart and would not wish you to hang.'

'You should know better than to try to bribe me, miss. He would kill me if I crossed him. Once you take his money, there's no going back—not if you value your life.'

'Very well, I shall not ask again.'

'I'm sorry, miss. No doubt your brother will pay well to have you back. Once the ransom is delivered, you'll be free to go home.'

If only she could believe him. However, there was no use in arguing further.

Jane said no more. As the door was closed and

locked behind him, she walked to the bed and sat down. She could only be glad that she had walked ahead of Lady Mary. Such an experience would have been too much for her godmother, who was no longer young, and she could not have escaped and left her a prisoner of the ruthless Blake.

Jane was determined not to give way to fear. She must find a way out of her prison.

Wandering over to the window, she looked down and saw that it was a long way from the ground. She could not see a tree or anything that might break her fall if she decided to jump. Yet she might attempt it if she became desperate. She lifted the catch. It moved easily enough, but the window would not budge. Investigating further, Jane saw that the wooden frame had been nailed through. Her captors were taking no chances this time.

Sighing, she sat on the edge of the bed. She would just have to wait for the morning until Blake came himself. Perhaps he would be reasonable. He must know that she was not an heiress, so what did he expect?

* * *

'I saw them snatch her, sir,' the Bow Street Runner told George. 'It took me by surprise. Everything looked right and tight. She got into the coach, willing like—but then he jumped in after her and they was off like the devil was after them. By the time I went after them they had disappeared, but I think they were heading for the river. I've got men out searching. There are a couple of places we are watching. We know the landlords as rogues. If she is in London, we'll find her, sir, don't you worry.'

'And if they have taken her out of London?'

'One of our men will question every turnpike on all the roads leaving town, my lord. Depend upon it that someone will have seen something.'

'I pray that you are right, sir.'

'Nobody gets away from Toby Price, my lord. It's my opinion the lady will have been taken south of the river—I've got a nose for these things, you'll see.'

'Next time you see the rogue, shoot to kill,' George said grimly. 'I would not have had this happen for the world. Jane has been abducted once. To have it happen again is more than any young woman should have to bear.'

'I dared not fire at the coachman, my lord. To do so might have caused an accident. It is my opinion that the young lady is in no immediate danger. If I'm not mistaken, the man who posed as her groom is someone known to us as Gentleman Starky. He was once a gentleman's gentleman and prides himself on his manners. I've put the word out on him. If he's seen, I'll know within hours.'

George could only accept his assurances that everything was being done to find Jane. However, he blamed himself for what had happened to her. By trying to arrest Blake, he had turned him into a dangerous fugitive. Now Jane's life could be at risk and there was little he could do except wait for news of her whereabouts.

He prayed that Blake would be desperate for money. If he was anxious for a ransom, Jane would not be harmed—but supposing he wanted revenge? He might kill her and worse.

The thought was too terrible to bear. George could not get the possibility out of his mind. He was unable to rest and sat in a wing chair in his library, staring at the dying embers of a fire his servants had thoughtfully lit.

If Jane were to die or be harmed by Blake, George would never forgive himself. He cared for her deeply, but this latest insult to her had made him fully aware of how unfit he was to offer her even friendship. He had botched the affair, miscalculating Blake's reactions. His actions had been meant to draw the rogue's fire on himself. Instead, he had endangered the woman he loved.

It had taken George a while to understand his heart, but now he saw clearly that Jane was the only woman he would ever wish to wed. He had blocked the knowledge from his mind, because it was unlikely to happen.

Jane would wish him to kingdom come and her brother had shown his disgust over the whole affair. George would not rest until Jane was found. Even if he could never marry her himself, he must know that she was safe and happy. If Blake had harmed her…but that way lay madness. He closed his eyes, dozing fitfully in the chair.

* * *

George's butler entered the next morning.

'Have you news for me?'

'Nothing yet, my lord. Would you have me bring water for you to shave?'

'Yes, I shall go up and change. If news comes, I am to be informed immediately.'

'Certainly, my lord. Should I have food brought to you upstairs?'

'Some bread and meat. If no news comes, I shall go out and search for her myself.'

'Forgive me for disturbing you, miss,' Stark apologised as he brought in a tray of bread, butter, cheese and a small mug of ale. 'I know this is not proper fare for a lady, but there is no tea or chocolate in the house. At least the bread is fresh.'

'Thank you,' Jane said as he set the tray down on the chest of drawers. It was morning and she had slept fitfully, her dreams uneasy and worrying. 'Do you think you could bring me some water to wash?'

'Yes, miss. I have it ready. I shall bring it up in a few minutes, but I thought you might be hungry.'

'You are thoughtful, sir. Tell me, what brought you to this life? I think you were not always used to such surroundings?'

'I worked for a gentleman and his family for all my life, miss. I was dismissed wrongly for theft. Accused of taking guineas that did not belong to me and dismissed without a reference. I tried to find honest work, but no one would employ me.'

'I would employ you,' Jane said. 'You told me not to attempt to bribe you—but if you could help me to escape, I would give you a position that would restore your good name.'

'It is kind of you to offer, miss. I wish I could help you—but Blake is vindictive. He would have my throat slit as soon as look at me.'

'Think about it,' Jane said as he opened the door and went out.

She took the tray to the bed and sat on the edge, breaking a piece of bread and spreading it with butter and a thin slice of cheese. The food was surprisingly good and she ate half of what had been provided, taking two sips of ale from the mug. Returning the tray to the top of the chest of drawers, she was behind the door when the door was unlocked and someone entered.

She knew at once that it was not Stark. A tingling sensation at the nape of her neck told her that this must be Captain Blake—the rogue who had abducted Mariah and her. Seizing the iron candlestick, she put her hand behind her back.

Blake swore as he saw the bed was unoccupied and swung round to stare at Jane.

'We meet again, sir,' she said, her heart racing. Inside, she was quaking, but outwardly she was determined to show no fear. 'I imagined I owed my present situation to your intervention. May I ask what you intend to do with me?'

'You and your family have interfered in my business once too often,' Blake said and scowled at her. His left arm was in a crude sling and it was obvious from the way he moved that he felt pain from his wound. 'Your brother tried to kill me and failed. It is as well for you that his shot went wide. Without me, my men would have panicked and you might have ended in the river. If I were a vengeful man, you would already be dead. However, I require money so that I can live abroad. Therefore, you are safe enough for the moment. If the ransom is paid, I shall allow you to live.'

'What exactly did my brother do to you?'

'He and that fool Marlowe tried to arrest me. Marlowe will pay the price for his treachery. I do not forgive those that betray me—but your brother may redeem himself by payment of forty thousand guineas.'

Jane could not control her gasp of dismay. 'Andrew could never afford so much. He would have to sell the estate and even then I do not think he could raise such a sum. You ask too much, sir.'

'If he does not have the money, he must get it from his rich friends—or he will never see you again.' Blake's gaze narrowed. 'What are you hiding behind your back?'

Jane's fingers tightened about the iron candle-stick. If he saw what she had, he would take it from her and any chance she had of escaping would be gone.

'Only this,' she said and moved towards him as she brought her arm out. 'You are a rogue, sir—and you mistook me for a foolish woman.'

Blake swore and grabbed at her arm, but Jane was too quick for him. She struck at the side of his head with her weapon, and, more from luck than judgement, her blow sent him to his knees with a curse. Immediately, Jane ran through the door, which Blake had left open when he entered. She slammed the door shut behind her and locked it.

Why Blake had been so careless she could not imagine, but, because she had been standing behind the door, he had seen only an empty room as he entered. Perhaps his mind was still a little fuddled from the night before or perhaps he had thought himself capable of dealing with a defenceless woman.

Behind her, Blake had risen to his feet and flung himself at the door. He was yelling and banging on it as she fled down the stairs to the hall below. She turned the handle of the front door and ran out into the inn yard. Hearing a cry of alarm behind her, she glanced back and saw the innkeeper in the doorway. He had a pistol aimed at her and at this distance he could not miss.

'Stop or I fire,' he yelled.

Jane felt a trickle of fear down her spine. She hesitated for a moment, then saw another man behind the innkeeper. Stark raised his arm and grabbed hold of the other man's wrist, twisting it so that he fired into the air.

Jane wasted no more time. She ran towards the nearest alley and fled into it. Stark had given her a few minutes' grace, but she knew that Blake's cries would have been heard. Someone would release him and then he would start searching for her.

She must run as far and as fast as she could and hope that she could lose herself in the maze of dirty little back streets that clustered at the water's edge.

Chapter Nine

'What news?' Andrew asked as George was admitted to Lady Mary's drawing room later that morning. 'I thought there might be a ransom note, but I have heard nothing as yet.'

'My Runner thinks he may have found her. He has men watching the back and the front of an inn south of the Thames, and someone on the inside. It is a place known to the Runners, the haunt of thieves and low life. Someone said a lady was taken there last night. Gentleman Starky was heard to argue with the landlord before she was hurried upstairs—and Price's informant says food was taken up to her later by Stark himself.'

'Who is Stark—or Starky?' Andrew said. 'You've lost me, Marlowe.'

'Stark was apparently a gentleman's gentleman,

hence the nickname. Price's informant says that he has been working for a rum cove recently. From the description, I would say he is Blake's man.'

'Then we have the rogues,' Andrew said, a look of grim satisfaction in his eyes. 'We must get Jane out of there—and bring Blake to account for his crimes. It is time he was safely in prison.'

'The sooner the better as far as I am concerned,' George agreed. 'But we must be careful. Price has men who are experienced in these matters. He says it would be best left to him. They will go in under pretence of searching for stolen goods. If Jane is there, they will bring her out.'

'How long will all that take? I want my sister back now, Marlowe. If news of this reaches the ears of the gossips, her reputation will suffer.'

'This unfortunate affair cannot be concealed,' George said and frowned. 'Lady Mary's hostess knew of the abduction and I dare say most of London will have heard whispers. If there is any danger of a scandal I should be honoured to do what I could to avert it.'

'What is that supposed to mean?' Andrew demanded. 'If you imagine I would consent to a match between you, you may dismiss it from your mind. My sister will not marry a man who is lucky not to be heading for the hangman's noose.'

'Damn you, Lanchester. If you were not Jane's brother, I should call you out for that—you know very well that I took part in Lady Fanshawe's abduction under a misapprehension. My offer of marriage was made in good faith.'

'And refused.' Andrew's expression gave nothing away. 'I am grateful for your help in this matter—but that does not mean I would allow my sister to—'

'Lord George, I am so glad to see you,' Lady Mary said as she came bustling into the room. 'Andrew, I have a letter for you—it was delivered by hand a few minutes ago. Do you think it is…?'

'The ransom?' Andrew finished for her and took the letter. He glanced at the scrawled writing. 'The hand is disguised, I have no doubt.' He tore the seal open and scanned the terse message. 'He demands forty thousand or I shall not see my sister again. Damn the rogue! I am not sure

I could raise such a sum at the moment, even if I sold my estate.'

'I can offer ten thousand pounds,' Lady Mary said instantly. 'Perhaps more if I have time to sell some property.'

'I would pay the ransom myself if necessary,' George said with authority. 'I can raise the money in a few days—but we should not give in to his demands, Lanchester. Be patient and give the Bow Street Runners a chance to get her back.'

'Where is the inn you think is Blake's hideout?' Andrew demanded. 'I wish to be there myself when this raid takes place.'

'That is the main reason I came here,' George replied in a manner as clipped and remote as Andrew's. 'We shall go together and take my carriage. If Jane is found, we must have some way of bringing her back discreetly.'

'Mrs Buxton promised to be discreet,' Lady Mary told them. 'I dare say there may be some scandal—it can hardly be forgotten—but I shall not allow it to interfere with my plans. Jane must not be treated as if she has done something disgraceful. It is my intention to take her to Bath as soon as she feels well enough to leave London.'

The two men looked at each other, but neither said what was on their minds. Fortunately, Lady Mary had no idea of how dangerous Blake truly was—and the fear that they would not recover Jane alive was reflected in their eyes as they left the house.

It must have been early in the morning when she fled the inn. The streets had been almost empty, apart from a milkmaid with a yoke across her shoulders and some ragged children huddled in doorways. Jane had seen no one as she began her flight through the dirty narrow back streets that bordered the docks. She passed warehouses, silent and derelict, and cottages that looked as if their tiny windows had never been washed, the paint peeled away from rotting wood. Here and there, a sleepy woman emerged from her front door to throw slops into the gutters; the stench was almost sufficient to make Jane vomit her breakfast.

At first she had expected to hear shouts as

Blake's men pursued her, but after a few minutes she felt calmer and began to walk swiftly rather than run. In this part of the great sprawling city, the lanes that backed onto the river resembled a warren, with courtyards filled with hovels sometimes built in such a way that it was impossible to pass and she had to turn back and look for another route.

As time passed more and more people were out on the streets. Most of them were dressed in clothes that Jane would describe as rags, their faces grey with dirt, their hair greasy and straggling about faces that were unnaturally pale. She became conscious that the people stared at her and saw resentment in their eyes. One man looked at her sullenly from the doorway of his hovel. As she met his suspicious gaze, he spat on the ground, narrowly missing her shoe.

Jane shivered. She was wearing a fine silk evening gown, her thin leather slippers already stained with the filth of the streets. At her throat was a string of pearls—its cost enough to feed these families for months.

Jane ran from the accusing stares, her heart racing madly. She had lost all sense of direction and had no idea where she was going. She might be heading back to the river and the inn for all she knew. Had she dared, she would have stopped to ask, but the menacing look in the eyes of the man who had spat at her had made her afraid to risk enquiring the way.

Pausing to catch her breath, she heard the noise of wheels on cobbles and her instinct told her to walk in the direction of the sound. Coming suddenly out of the maze of lanes, she found herself in a much broader thoroughfare and sighed with relief. Here, the people were normal workmen and maids hurrying about their business.

She looked farther ahead and saw a hackney cab drawn up at the side of the road. She ran towards it, calling out as the man turned his head to look at her.

'Please,' she begged. 'Can you take me to Russell Street, sir? I shall pay you when we get there.'

He eyed her suspiciously for a moment, then inclined his head. 'You look as if you can afford the fare. What are you doing, staying out all night, miss?'

'That is a long story,' Jane said, her cheeks warm. 'I need to get home as quickly as possible. Lady Mary's butler will pay you twice your fare, sir, if you take me at once...'

'You'd best get in then, miss. It ain't right that a young lady like you should be wandering the streets in a place like this—and I'd be failing in me duty if I didn't look out for you. My Betty would tell me off good and proper if I left you here at the mercy of folks round here.'

'Thank you. I am so grateful.' Jane climbed into his carriage and instructed the driver where to go before she sat back with her eyes closed as it began to move off. Tears began to trickle down her cheeks. At the inn she had managed to control her fear, but her flight through the rookery of dirty streets had exhausted her courage. All she wanted now was to be at home with her godmother.

It was all very well being an independent woman, but there were times when it would be nice to lean one's head against a strong shoulder and be comforted.

* * *

'My men made a thorough search of the place,' Price told them. 'They found this stole, which may belong to Miss Lanchester—but neither she nor Blake were there.'

Andrew took the spangled stole and frowned. 'My sister has one similar, but I would have to ask Lady Mary if she was wearing it last night.'

George took the stole and held it to his nose. 'It smells of her perfume. I would swear it is hers. You are certain they were not hiding her in a cellar or the attics?'

'My men are thorough, sir. I can assure you that everywhere was checked.' The Runner hesitated, then, 'We found some blood on an iron candlestick in one of the bedrooms—and there was a bloodstained coat in the kitchen. The landlord has been taken to Newgate prison and will be questioned, but at the moment he refuses to answer.'

'He will answer to me,' Andrew said fiercely. 'If my sister has been murdered, he will swing for it.'

'Leave this rascal to me,' George said. 'We do not yet know what happened here. They may have realised they were being watched and taken Jane elsewhere.'

'They may have rumbled us,' Price agreed. 'My informant has gone missing. I'm wondering if it is his blood on that coat. I think it unlikely they killed Miss Lanchester. If the motive was money, they would need her alive.'

'I will go to the prison,' George said. 'Go home, Lanchester, and see if there is news of your sister. The kidnapper may have sent you another demand.'

'Your fellows have bungled this affair,' Andrew said unfairly. 'I have wasted too much time already. I must somehow raise the money to pay for Jane's return.'

'I have told you that I can find it within a few days,' George replied stiffly. 'Since this all came about because of a mistake I made, I insist that you allow me to pay.'

'We'll keep looking, sir,' Price said. 'If they've taken the young lady elsewhere, you may depend on it that someone will have seen something.'

'Jane, my dearest child,' Lady Mary exclaimed as she entered her godmother's parlour. She had taken off her filthy shoes, giving them to the footman who admitted her to dispose of, and her feet were bare. 'Where have you been? We have all been so worried about you.'

'I have asked your footman to pay the driver of a hackney cab, ma'am. I promised him double his fare for bringing me home. I hope that is all right?'

'Of course, my love. You have no need to ask.' Lady Mary had risen and moved swiftly towards her. She embraced Jane, then looked into her face. 'You are shaking. Are you cold?'

'I left my stole behind when I escaped.' Jane caught back a sob. 'It was so awful. I ran away, but the people in those lanes were so wretched and they stared at me...' She began to cry, unable to hold back her emotion. 'He said he would kill me if the ransom was not paid and I hit him. He was careless and left the door unlocked and I ran out and locked him in, and then the horrible man with a squint would have shot me if Stark hadn't knocked his arm and...'

'You are overwrought, dearest, and no wonder.' Lady Mary put an arm about her, thoroughly bewildered by the rambling tale. 'You have been through far more than any young woman should have to bear. If your brother had told me that you were in danger, I should have had more grooms to guard us when we went out.'

'It wasn't your fault.' Jane raised her head, brushing a hand over her face to wipe away the tears. The words tumbled out of her thick and fast. 'If you had not lingered on the doorstep, they would have grabbed you, too. He had a pistol and I could not jump from the carriage because of its speed. I begged Stark to help me, but he was afraid of Blake, but then at the end he stopped that awful man shooting me. I dare not think what they may have done to him.'

'I fear you go too fast for me,' Lady Mary said. 'I am going to take you upstairs. You must have a nice wash and then get into bed, my love. I shall have the doctor fetched to you and—'

'I do not need the doctor, Godmother. I will do as you say and rest, but please do not send for the doctor. The fewer people that know of this, the better.'

'I fear the gossips will already have heard,'

Lady Mary told her and smiled. 'You should not be too concerned for your reputation, dearest. I am certain there is a simple way to rectify any scandal.'

'I do not think it will be so simple,' Jane said and shook her head. 'I am too tired to think now. I hardly slept last night. I should like a dish of tea when I am in bed, if it is no trouble.'

'You run along and make yourself comfortable,' Lady Mary said. 'I am happy that you are home and that the situation is no worse, Jane. When you feel rested, we shall go down to Bath and put all this upset behind us.'

Jane inclined her head and went up the stairs. Her godmother seemed to think they should just go on as before, but at the moment all Jane wanted to do was to go somewhere quiet and forget.

'She hit the cove what had her brung to me house,' Rab muttered sullenly. He rubbed at his wrist. George had him in an iron grip that had forced him to his knees and the pistol pointed at his head had a remarkable effect on loosening his tongue. 'You had no call to do that, sir. It weren't me as had 'er snatched. When he says do summat, it gets done or things happen.'

'Thus far you have escaped lightly,' George said in a deceptively pleasant tone. 'If I discover you are lying to me, you will pray that your hanging comes soon, my friend.'

'Don't hurt me again.' The innkeeper's face turned yellow with fear. 'I swear it is as I told yer. He must 'ave left the door open when he went in ter the room she was locked in—she took a chance and hit him and then escaped.'

'And no one tried to stop her?'

'There were a bit of an altercation between me and Stark,' Rab admitted. 'It were his fault she got away. Blake went mad and they had a fight, but the cap'n come off worst fer once, 'cos he had a sore shoulder—and bled all over his coat. Stark went orf. Said he wouldn't work for the devil no more and when he sorted himself out, the cap'n went orf in a rare temper.'

'Then you do not know where she is?'

'I ain't got no idea. It weren't my fault she was taken, me lord. I only done what I were told.'

'I dare say you took money for it. You are as guilty as any of them and should hang for your crime.'

'Yer said yer would help me if I told yer the truth.'

'You must pray that Miss Lanchester is alive when we find her,' George said, his mouth tight with anger. 'You may then escape with transportation. If she is harmed in any way, you will hang for your part in this business.'

'Damn yer,' Rab muttered. 'Yer all the same, bloody aristocrats—arrogant bastards the lot of yer.'

'I may well be arrogant,' George said, 'but I keep my word. If Miss Lanchester is found alive and unharmed, I shall do my best to see that your sentence is lighter than it would otherwise be.'

George signalled to the gaoler and was allowed to leave the cell. He breathed deeply as he went out into the fresh air. The stench of Newgate was too well remembered from his previous visit here and a part of him sympathised with the rascally innkeeper. Yet the man had no doubt played his role in this business willingly for money.

The rogue who had snatched Lady Fanshawe and Jane was the man who deserved the ultimate punishment. Blake must hang for what he had done.

George's lips thinned as he strode through the streets. He would go straight to Lady Mary's house. He must tell her and Jane's brother what he had discovered.

'Jane is here?' Andrew looked at his sister's godmother, then put a hand to his face in relief. He sat down in a chair opposite her. 'Thank God for it! Where is she? I need to know exactly what happened.'

'Jane is in bed. When I looked in on her she was sleeping. My housekeeper made her a tisane and I think it soothed her. She was very distressed. Overwrought, I should say.'

'Yes. It was a terrible experience for her.' Andrew's expression was grim. 'Did she tell you anything?'

'Some garbled tale of having struck someone and escaped. I really could not make head or tale of it, Andrew. I am sure she will explain it all to you when she has reco—' Lady Mary stopped speaking as the door of her parlour opened and the housekeeper entered. 'Yes, Mrs Scott?'

'Lord George is here, ma'am. He asked to see you or Lord Lanchester.'

'Oh, tell him to come in,' Lady Mary said. 'We have excellent news.'

Jane woke, yawned and stretched. She had not slept for very long, but the rest had refreshed her, settling her nerves. The kidnap and imprisonment in the inn had not distressed her as much as her escape. The way some of those wretched people had looked at her as she became lost in a maze of dark alleys had been frightening. She had not realised that such awful places existed.

Although she had heard of the terrible slums in parts of London, she had never before seen them for herself. The utter despair she had witnessed had been a shock and a revelation for her. Her own brush with the underworld had made her realise what hopeless lives the people in those lanes must live and her heart had been touched. She had found her brief experience horrifying. What must it be like for women and children forced to live in such an environment?

Jane could only imagine what kind of things went on in the derelict houses and inns she had seen during her flight. If she could be held captive at the whim of one man, how many other young women were forced into lives of degradation and shame? And what of the children she had seen huddling in doorways?

In thinking of others, she had pushed her own distress to a small corner of her mind, where it must remain. Jane was too sensible a girl to let her abduction play on her mind, even though she understood she must be very careful in future.

As she approached her aunt's parlour, she saw the door was partially open and she could hear the sound of voices from inside.

'Jane is safe now and that is all that I care for,' Lady Mary said. 'This squabbling between you two must cease for her sake. As soon as she is well enough, I shall take Jane to Bath. If you wish to arrange some kind of surveillance for her safety, that is your business, Andrew, but I will not have her shuffled off abroad as if she has done something wrong.'

'The tales are everywhere,' Andrew said, and Jane could tell that he was angry. 'I was asked twice this morning if it was true that you and she had eloped together.'

'And what did you say?' Lord George answered. 'It would have stopped their tongues at once if you had told them we are engaged.'

'Now that is a handsome offer, in my opinion,' Lady Mary cried. 'You must see that Jane's reputation may suffer, Andrew? Surely it makes sense to accept Lord George's offer? Jane likes him well enough—and left to herself she may never marry.'

'My sister has no need to marry unless she wishes,' Andrew replied. 'I have no desire to see her wed to a rogue.'

'Andrew!' Lady Mary exclaimed. 'Have a care. You should not insult a fellow gentleman.'

'I would call you out,' George replied, 'if I could be bothered—but you are behaving like a spoiled schoolboy. I am extremely fond of your sister—and it would be a sensible solution. As my wife, Jane would be accepted in the best society. Any scandal would be swept under the carpet and it is the honourable solution…'

'Damn you, my sister does not need your charity.'

'Why do you not let Jane decide for herself?' Lady Mary suggested.

This was so humiliating, to hear them squabbling over her future as if she were something shameful to be brushed under the carpet.

Having heard more than enough, Jane pushed the door wide and walked in. She raised her head, her cheeks hot as she saw their guilty looks.

'Thank you, Godmother,' she said with remarkable dignity. 'I am old enough to make my own decision, which is that I shall go to Bath with you.' Her eyes turned on Andrew proudly. She was every inch the capable and calm lady of independent means. 'I believe I have no need of your permission if I wished to marry, Andrew.'

'Well, no, but the fellow helped kidnap Lady Fanshawe. You cannot wish to marry him, Jane?'

One glance from her speaking eyes caused him to fall silent.

'I do not consider that I have done anything that makes it imperative for me to marry to save my reputation. Whomever or whether I wish to marry is my affair and mine alone.' Her gaze fell on George; it did not become any warmer. 'I am most grateful for your generous offer, sir. However, I think your gallantry misplaced. As Lady Mary will tell you, I have never had the intention of marrying. Nothing that has happened recently makes the slightest difference.'

'Miss Lanchester—Jane—how are you?' George asked, his gaze moving over her with concern. 'I have been told of your escape and I was delighted to discover that you were safely home. Once again you faced a difficult situation bravely. I cannot tell you how glad I am that you were not harmed.'

'You are good to be concerned, sir.'

George's expression did not change a fraction, his gaze unwavering.

'I am sorry you should have overheard a foolish exchange with your brother. I fear that both of us are guilty of speaking out of turn. I quite understand your reasons for not wishing to accept my offer—but I assure you it was made for the right reasons and not charity, as Lanchester suggests.'

'I know you to be a generous man.' Jane spoke stiffly because inside she was hurting. She had been placed in an impossible situation and there was only one way of dealing with the embarrass-ment of having heard their quarrel. 'However, I see no reason for you to offer marriage out of a sense of duty, sir. I shall save you the trouble of asking. It would not suit me to be married at the moment.'

'Jane dearest,' Lady Mary said, 'you might wish to speak to Lord George privately about this. Come, Andrew, I think we should leave them together.'

'No, Godmother, please do not leave. I shall show Lord George to the door. We may say all that we wish before he leaves.'

'You will be wishing me to the devil,' George said. 'Pray do not trouble yourself to see me out, Miss Lanchester. I am not worthy of your notice and shall try not to impose on your society in fu-ture. Ma'am, Lanchester, excuse me.'

Jane felt the tears sting her eyes as he walked from the room. He was angry. Her answer had made him believe that she disliked him and Andrew's behaviour had been nothing less than rude. She wanted to apologise, but her pride would not let her.

She turned reproachful eyes on her brother. 'I hope you are pleased with yourself, Andrew. You have insulted Lord George once too often.'

'Jane…' Andrew stared at her face. Something of what she was feeling must have got through to him, for he looked ashamed. 'You could not wish to marry him? Not after what he did?'

'He saved my life and he rescued Mariah. Had I not escaped, I dare say he would have done his best to find me this time.'

'He paid Bow Street Runners to search for you,' Lady Mary said. 'And he offered to pay the forty-thousand-pound ransom if it was needed. I think he cares for you a great deal, Jane.'

'He is a gentleman of honour, no matter what Andrew thinks,' Jane said, her throat hoarse as she struggled against her emotion. 'What he offered was exactly what I would have expected of him. You were insufferably rude to him, Andrew.'

Andrew looked uncomfortable. 'I was angry. I did not imagine that you cared for him, Jane.'

'I do not,' Jane said and left the room quickly before the tears could fall.

Behind her, Lady Mary and Andrew looked at each other in silence for a moment, then, 'I didn't think she really cared for him,' he said.

'She is in love with him,' Lady Mary said and shook her head at his frown. 'The best thing you can do, Andrew, is to take yourself off to your estate and leave your sister to me. Her pride is sadly bruised. Jane has borne her ordeal bravely but her emotions are in tatters. She needs to come to terms with her feelings. Lord George may decide that it is worth making another push to win her, but if he does not I must see what I can do to bring them together.'

'Are you saying I should allow them to marry?'

'Jane is old enough to decide for herself. She would wish for your blessing, but, if she once made up her mind, I do not think you could stop her.'

'No, perhaps not. If she can twice escape from a rogue like Blake, she is capable of choosing her own husband.' Andrew ran his fingers through his dark hair. 'I suppose I was a bit rough on Marlowe. I have something of a temper.'

'You were fortunate he did not call you out. You should write a short note of apology—but say nothing of Jane. If Jane believes she is being coerced into a marriage to save her reputation, she will refuse it—as she did just now.'

'Why did she—if she cares for him?'

'She was embarrassed. Put yourself in her place, Andrew.'

'I dare say you are right.' He was rueful. 'I shall apologise to Jane later—but Blake remains a danger. I must do something about protecting my sister.'

'I think you may safely leave that to Lord George. He told you it was his intention to employ men to watch over her. Write and accept his offer of help in the matter of Jane's protection—and apologise. I shall make certain he is informed of any slight danger to her safety. Perhaps, when they meet again, they will come to their senses and admit their love for each other and then you must accept their marriage with a smile.'

'You mean that you will find a way of bring-ing him to Bath if he does not come of his own accord?'

'Exactly so.'

'You are a very wise lady,' Andrew said. 'Excuse me, I shall write the letter at once.'

Jane was shaken by a storm of tears. She leaned against the door of her room and then locked it, not wanting to be disturbed. Her distress and embarrassment at hearing her brother and Lord George argue over her was acute. Andrew had been abominably rude, but that was not the worst of it. To hear him say that his sister did not re-quire Lord George's charity had cut her to the quick. What must have passed between them be-fore her arrival?

What had Lord George said to make her brother deny him in such terms? Was her reputation so completely ruined that Lord George felt obliged to marry her? Clearly he had no wish for it or they would not have been discussing her in such a manner.

It was so lowering! She could not bear that he

felt he must marry her. Andrew must have accused him of bringing her reputation into ill repute. Indeed, his insults might have demanded satisfaction had not Lord George been so forbearing.

It was simply not his fault that she had been kidnapped the first time. Jane knew that her reckless nature had led her into trouble and she had only herself to blame for what had happened. Blake had told her that he had had her abducted out of a desire for revenge the second time, and that was as much her brother's fault as Lord George's. Jane's own bravery had accomplished her recent escape, but on the first occasion she owed much to her rescuer.

She was in love with Lord George and, had he asked because he cared for her, she would have been happy to cast independence to the winds in favour of love, even though she might be making a terrible mistake for a woman of her nature. Yet knowing that she cared for him made the humiliation so much harder to bear. He had asked out of a sense of duty—because her brother had blamed him for ruining her reputation.

* * *

George stared moodily out of the window. It had just started to drizzle with rain, which, on top of the way he was feeling, was highly depressing. He knew that he ought to have expected Lanchester's anger at his proposal. What brother in his right mind would wish to see his sister married to a man who was the cause of her abduction?

He kicked moodily at an inoffensive and very attractive music stand. Jane had been very dignified, but she had looked pale and was clearly in distress. It was no wonder after what she had been through. Having been to the inn where she was held captive, George knew what it must have been like for her in the surrounding lanes and alleys. Alone and fleeing for her life, she must have been terrified.

How brave and beautiful she was. He could hardly fault her for refusing his proposal. George knew himself unworthy—yet he could not help a tiny spark of hope flaring. Something in her eyes had told him a very different story.

He had avoided speaking to her alone, knowing that she must have heard what was being said and would not understand. He had offered because his own feelings were involved, but had couched his offer to her brother in a way he thought Lanchester might find acceptable. Well, it had backfired on him and now he must think again.

One thing he was determined on. That rogue Blake would not be allowed to come near Jane again. She would be watched every time she left her home and Price's men had been told to shoot to kill. Jane must be protected whatever the consequences.

Perhaps one day, when she had had time to recover from her distress, she might find it in her heart to forgive him for what had happened to her.

Chapter Ten

'Do you feel able to attend Lady Astley's ball?' Lady Mary asked two days later. 'It may be an ordeal for you, my love, because the gossips will have heard something—but I think it should be attempted, if you can.'

'I shall certainly attend,' Jane said, lifting her head to meet her godmother's anxious gaze. 'If anyone asks me, I shall tell them the truth—at least I shall say that I was abducted and held to ransom. However, the rest shall remain our secret.'

'I think you are wise, dearest. Some of the strictest hostesses may cut you from their list, but that must be accepted. We cannot reverse what has happened to you, Jane, but if you act properly it is my belief that most will think you a heroine. This will be our last engagement in town, for we shall go down to Bath the day after tomorrow. I have many friends there and I assure you, you will not be ostracised there whatever happens this evening.'

'I have no reason to be ashamed,' Jane said, 'yet I would not bring disgrace on you, Godmother. If we meet with criticism in Bath, I shall go home.'

'Do you imagine that anyone who cut you would remain my friend?' Lady Mary looked affronted. 'You are very precious to me, dearest. I shall support you to the last. Indeed, those who malign you do so at their peril. I am not without influence and I should use it in your support. Some might find themselves being excluded from certain circles.'

Jane's eyes felt damp. It meant everything to have her godmother's staunch support, because she knew that girls in similar cases had been rushed abroad by their embarrassed families or forced into a convenient marriage—some might even be sent to a house of correction, though it was not their fault.

Her throat caught as she remembered the quarrel she had heard between Andrew and Lord George. If her hot-tempered brother had not denied him, she might never have known anything about his gallant offer. He would most certainly have disguised his reasons for asking her and she might well have accepted his offer of marriage.

Jane was aware of a deep searing regret. How happy she might have been had Lord George truly wished to marry her for his own sake.

Forcing the regret to a tiny corner of her mind, Jane prepared for the evening ahead. She had been quite popular at the dances they attended, sitting out only a few times. This evening she might discover that she had far fewer friends than she believed.

Lady Astley welcomed them to her house, giving no sign that she had heard any gossip concerning Jane. Moving on into the crowded reception rooms, Jane felt a fluttering in her stomach. She sensed that most eyes in the room were upon her and for a moment it seemed that a hush descended. Her nails curled into the palms of her hands as the hush was replaced by a buzz of voices and she heard some of the whispers as she passed by.

'An elopement gone wrong, do you think?' one woman said in a slightly too-loud voice, only to be shushed by her husband.

'I heard she was abducted and escaped from the rogues without assistance,' a gentleman told his wife. 'In my opinion, Jane Lanchester is a very brave young lady.'

'I should not dare to show my face in public if such a thing had happened to me…'

'It shows great resilience on her part…'

Jane managed to keep a show of unconcern on her face. Lady Mary stopped to speak to some friends and Jane smiled, inclining her head in response to enquiries about her health.

'I am very well, thank you, ma'am,' Jane replied with dignity. 'I was a little frightened, but quite unharmed.'

'Then it is true? You were abducted?' The lady seemed astonished that she was prepared to admit it.

'I believe I must have been mistaken for an heiress,' Jane said in a calm clear voice that people standing nearby could hear. 'My brother was asked for an impossible ransom, but I was able to escape and he was not forced to ruin himself for my sake.'

'Oh, I say, bravo, Miss Lanchester,' Sir Tobin Marshall said and clapped his hands. 'May I hope that you will grant me the favour of two dances this evening? I should like to hear more of your remarkable adventures. It is the duty of all gentlemen to stand up to these rogues and see they pay the price for such infamy.'

'I could not agree more,' a voice that made Jane's pulses race joined in. 'You will please save two dances for me, Miss Lanchester.'

Jane glanced at Lord George. His smile was warm and approving and she felt relieved. He was not angry with her. She handed her card to Sir Tobin and then to Lord George, feeling grateful for their kindness. Their outspoken support had brought a small queue of gentlemen to request a dance and it was not long before at least two-thirds of her card was filled.

'Thank you for helping to rescue me,' Jane said as she danced with Lord George later. 'I was not sure you would be here this evening—and I thought you might be angry with me. I believe I was a little abrupt with you the other night.'

'I have no reason to be angry with you,' George said and it seemed to her that his eyes held a smile for her alone. 'Your brother was just in his anger against me, Jane. I understood his feelings—and yours—but you must know in your heart that I did not speak out of duty.'

'You did not?' Jane's heart raced. 'I thought...' Her cheeks were warm and her heart was racing wildly. 'May I ask why you did speak, sir?'

'That is a matter for private discussion,' George said. 'If I called on you at eleven tomorrow morning, would you grant me a few minutes of your time?'

Jane hesitated, then inclined her head. 'Yes, sir. I should be happy to do so.'

'Then we shall continue our discussion tomorrow. This evening you must dance with everyone and give the gossips no reason for spite, Jane. I would not have you feel coerced in any way.'

'Thank you.' She gave him a tremulous smile. It was quite foolish of her, but her eyes pricked with tears. 'Lady Mary thought I might be ostracised this evening, but we believed it a risk worth taking.'

'Your godmother is a very wise lady,' George said. 'You have done nothing to be ashamed of, Jane. I think you as courageous as you are beautiful.'

'I would not think of myself as either brave or beautiful,' Jane said and laughed. 'Attractive, perhaps—but I am not a beauty.'

'You must let me be the judge,' George said. 'I am persuaded you are not in the habit of looking much in the mirror. Your eyes reach into a man's soul, Jane.'

Jane was lost for words, her cheeks warm. The music ended then and she glanced at him shyly as he returned her to her aunt. Almost immediately, she was claimed by another partner. George left her to join a party of friends, many of them gentlemen who had asked her for a dance earlier.

As the evening progressed, Jane was aware of coolness from more than one lady present, though the gentlemen seemed universally on her side.

She was not allowed to sit out one dance, and at supper she and Lady Mary were surrounded by gentlemen. One or two of their closest female friends joined the party.

Jane danced again with Lord George. Afterwards, he kissed her hand and reminded her of their appointment the next day.

Lady Mary had nodded her head, but made no comment until they were in the carriage being driven home later that evening.

'Well, it all seemed to go very well, dearest. Better than we might have hoped, which was due to Sir Tobin and Lord George to a great degree.'

'Both gentlemen were very kind, Godmother.'

'Yes, indeed. However, I think your honesty and deportment had much to do with it, Jane. One lady told me that she had been inclined to think there was some truth in the rumour of an elopement, but this evening she realised that you were too sensible a gal to behave so recklessly. And I had a message from one of the prince's aides, telling me that we are both invited to visit Carlton House when we return to London.'

'How kind of his Royal Highness—and your friend.' Jane smiled. 'You speak of my bravery, Godmother, but you also took a risk. You could have lost a great deal by being seen to condone my shame.'

'I did not consider it,' Lady Mary said not quite truthfully.

'I can only thank you,' Jane said and waited. Her godmother made no further comment. 'Lord George is to call on me in the morning.'

'Is he, my dear? He will wish to say good-bye before we leave town, I dare say.' A little smile touched Lady Mary's mouth, but she said no more.

Jane smiled and leaned back against the squabs. Her godmother was resisting the question and her tact was appreciated. Jane believed that she might have some news for Lady Mary after the visit, but it would be immodest to speak before she was certain.

She yawned behind her hand. 'I believe I shall sleep very well tonight. I am exhausted by all that dancing.'

'I have not danced, but I believe I shall rest tonight,' Lady Mary agreed and touched her hand. 'You know that all I want is your happiness, my dear. I would not persuade you to anything you did not want.'

Jane dressed in a simple but elegant grey silk gown. She fastened a large cameo brooch at her throat and touched her hair, which was caught up in a knot at her nape. Her hands fluttered nervously. Supposing she had been mistaken? Supposing Lord George did not truly care for her? Yet he knew her feelings. He would not ask her again simply out of duty, surely?

The longcase clock in the hall was striking a quarter to the hour. She took a deep breath and went downstairs to the front parlour. Picking up a book of her favourite poems, she tried to read a few lines, but found it impossible. After that dreadful scene when she interrupted a quarrel between her brother and Lord George, she had thought all her hopes at an end, but now…

'Miss Lanchester.' The housekeeper's words broke into her thoughts. 'A gentleman to see you—Lord George?'

'Yes, I am expecting Lord George,' Jane replied and rose to her feet, clasping her hands before her. 'Please show him in.'

'Yes, miss.'

Jane breathed deeply as the housekeeper went away. She was so very nervous!

In another moment Lord George walked into the room. He looked extremely elegant, his cravat arranged in an elegant waterfall, his blue coat moulded to his shoulders and his breeches a delicate shade of cream. Her gaze flew to his face and the look she saw there made her heart pound. She looked down, studying the shine on his boots.

'Jane, you are well?'

'Yes, very well, thank you, sir.' She dipped a small curtsy. 'I trust you are recovered from the wound to your shoulder?'

'As if it had never been.' He took a step towards her. 'I think you know why I have come.'

'I am not certain. You know my feelings on the matter of your making me an offer out of a mistaken desire to protect my reputation.'

'I think any rumours were nipped in the bud last night, do you not think so?'

'I believe so, sir.'

'Then I think we need not consider a marriage of obligation on either side. Indeed, I have not come to ask you to marry me this morning.'

'Oh.' Jane blushed. 'Forgive me…'

'Please do not be embarrassed. It was my intention to ask if you would accept me as your suitor. I think you must know that I have a high regard for you. If we discover that we enjoy each other's company sufficiently, it is my hope that you might listen to an offer in time.'

'Oh…' Jane stammered, her heart racing. 'Yes, I see. I think that would suit me well, sir.'

'I believe we shall suit, Jane. I think you're exactly the sort of lady I had hoped to wed one day. My sister and mother—much as I love them—are clinging vines. You are a lady of spirit, a lady I think might be as much a companion as a lover.'

Jane's heart soared. His words were music to her ears—it was exactly the kind of marriage she had hoped to find.

'I think that might please me very well, sir—

as long as you are certain that you do not feel obliged to offer.'

'I am quite certain. I shall take it that we have an understanding, though not yet an engagement?'

Jane nodded, her cheeks warm. 'If you wish.'

'I do not wish you to be coerced into anything by your very charming godmother—and I have yet to win your brother's approval.'

'Andrew will approve once he knows you. He needs a little time to accustom himself to the idea.'

'As you do?' George's smile made her heart race. 'I know I do not deserve your regard after the way I behaved at the start, but I hope to earn it in time.'

'Please, do not,' Jane said and put her fingers to his lips. 'You must not abuse yourself to me, my lord. You have nothing to apologise for in my opinion. I know how much you risked for my sake. You acted impulsively for another's sake and became involved in an unworthy act—but, had you not done what you did, both

Lady Fanshawe and I would have been in terrible trouble.'

'You are too generous, Jane,' George said. 'I know I do not deserve your love—but may I hope that you care a little? You have said more than once that you had no wish to marry.'

'I was not sure that I should find anyone who would be a friend and companion as well as a husband. I am used to ordering my own life. While I realise that marriage must change things, I should not like to become one of those wives who dare not answer back and fear to displease their husband if the cook throws a tantrum.'

'God forbid! I should hate such a marriage. You must never be afraid to speak your mind to me.'

'I think you really mean that.'

'What is in your mind?'

'I believe we should allow the world to think us at least close to making a match, if not actually engaged. While Blake is in hiding he remains a danger to us all. If he thought we were to marry…'

'You think it would draw him out.'

'He would wish to be revenged on us. He might do something reckless and reveal his hand.'

'You understand the danger?'

'Yes, of course. What is our alternative? If we wait and pretend we are no more than friends, we shall never be at ease. Only when he is caught shall we be certain we can live our lives safely without fear of being suddenly murdered by our enemy.'

'You are very brave, Jane.'

'I know that you will have me constantly watched and protected. In Bath I shall take care never to walk alone. Whatever we do, he remains a danger until he is caught.'

'Then the matter is settled. I shall escort you and Lady Mary to Bath and then visit your brother at his regiment's present posting in Devon. We shall allow the world to think we intend to wed. Should you wish to change your mind once you know me a little better, I shall not think the less of you.'

'I shall make the same offer to you,' Jane said with a hint of mischief in her face. 'Once Captain Blake has been dealt with, we shall speak of these matters again. However, I believe you should speak to my brother and make him aware of our possible intentions.'

'Would you allow me to kiss you?'

'I seem to recall that you needed no permission the last times…'

George laughed and reached for her, his lips caressing and exploring hers in a leisurely fashion that gave them both pleasure. Jane kissed him back in a manner that showed she was prepared to give as much as she received.

'I believe you are a tease, Miss Lanchester. May I take this to mean that you have forgiven me?'

'I was only angry with you for a very short time,' she murmured. 'Yet you are right. We hardly know one another. Something a few weeks as an engaged couple should put right.'

'I imagined you must have a dislike of me after what had happened. Indeed, I knew myself unworthy of you, Jane.'

'From the very beginning you were considerate of my welfare,' Jane told him. 'You have shown in so many ways that you are a man to be trusted and respected. You need not ask for forgiveness ever again. We are to be friends and equals, which means there is no need to say sorry.'

'My wonderful Jane. I think we shall suit very well,' George said, his hand at her nape. His fingers caressed her, sending a tingling sensation down her spine. She thought he would kiss her again, but he merely smiled. 'I shall bring you an engagement ring and—' He broke off and moved back one step as the door opened and Lady Mary walked in.

Her gaze went from one to the other; then she nodded, looking well pleased. 'So you have settled it all between you. I am so pleased for you both. I knew from the first that you would suit very well. May I wish you both happy?'

'Thank you, dearest Godmother,' Jane said. 'Had it not been for you, I might not have attended the ball last evening—and then this might never have happened.'

'I intended to come to you in Bath when things had settled a little,' George said. 'But Lady Mary was good enough to let me know that you would attend the ball last night and so all was well.'

Jane's smile faded. 'You wrote to him?'

'Lord George is arranging your protection, dearest,' Lady Mary replied serenely. 'It was necessary that he should know where you would be. The man who abducted you is still at large and we do not wish for another such attempt.'

'Lady Mary is perfectly right. You must be protected until Blake is caught, Jane.' George took her hand. 'Please do not imagine that I came here as a duty. Everything I have said is the truth.'

'I believe you.'

'Then we shall go on as we planned.' His smile sent tingles down her spine. 'So it is settled. We shall all travel to Bath in the morning, and then, when you are in residence at Lady Mary's home, I shall visit Andrew.'

'That sounds very satisfactory to me.' Lady Mary pulled on the bell rope. 'I shall send for some champagne so that we can celebrate.' She beamed at her goddaughter. 'This is one of the happiest days of my life, my love. I shall enjoy helping to plan your wedding. Shall you have it in Bath or at your home?'

'I think we should wait until Andrew comes to Bath,' Jane said. 'We shall decide then what suits us all.'

* * *

Jane thought that she had never enjoyed a journey as much. She rode in the carriage with Lady Mary until they were out of town, but once the they were in open countryside, George suggested that she might like to ride with him. He had brought horses with them, which the grooms surrendered, and after helping her to mount the horse he had thoughtfully provided with a side saddle, George mounted his own favourite stallion.

'He carried us both the last time we rode together,' George said, looking at her with mischief in his eyes, 'but now you have your own mount, Jane. Would you care to race for a while?'

'I should love it,' she said, accepting his challenge and spurring her horse to a gallop. 'Catch me if you can.'

Her challenge was accepted with alacrity and in no time he was riding by her side, pacing his horse so that they were in unison, enjoying the feeling of the wind in their faces and the freedom of the open road.

Jane knew that he could pass her if he wished

but it was enough for him to ride at her side and relish the thrill of the powerful horses that carried them.

Afterwards, when they rested the horses and waited for the carriage with Lady Mary to catch up, George held her hand and gazed into her eyes.

'We've had so little time to enjoy ourselves, Jane, but I think it would take a lifetime to know you.'

'What could be better?' she asked, laughter in her eyes. 'We have all the time in the world to discover each other's secrets.'

'Do you have secrets, Jane?'

'Perhaps,' she said. 'But I shan't tell you—you must discover them for yourself.'

'You little wretch,' George said and grabbed her, kissing her soundly. 'Where is your ticklish spot? I shall make you tell me...'

'Here comes the carriage,' Jane said. 'I think I should ride with my godmother or she will worry.'

'Another time...' George said and smiled, then touched her cheek. 'It is so good to see you laugh.'

Jane touched his hand, leaving him as she went back to the carriage. For a short time she'd forgotten all her problems, but the shadow was still there at her shoulder. Until Blake was captured or dead she could never be certain that either of them was safe.

'You must not worry about me,' Jane said and kissed George's cheek. 'We agreed that you should visit Andrew so that he understands what is going on and that must be your first priority. I shall be perfectly safe here in Bath. I know that I must be careful and I promise I shall not walk alone.'

'I know you are sensible,' George said, touching her cheek with his fingertips. 'I wish you did not have this shadow hanging over you at this time. I want you to be happy, dearest.'

'I am not afraid of Blake and I shall not let the thought of him overshadow my pleasure in our understanding,' Jane assured him. 'However, you must promise me that you will take care, George. Blake hates you and Andrew, but I think you will be his main target. You have ruined all his plans to gain a fortune. I dare say he is planning his revenge.'

'Yes, I know it,' George said and looked grave. 'I would that he were in prison where he belongs. It is not for want of trying, Jane. There is a warrant for his arrest in London, but I think he will be miles away from the city now.'

'Yes, perhaps. Yet, how can he know where I am?' Jane said. 'Do not let your anxiety for me cloud your thinking, George. It is most likely that he will have gone back to his old haunts— or perhaps abroad. If the news of our plans does not bring him out of hiding, I think we may forget him and get on with our lives.'

'Yes, you are right,' he agreed. 'Yet I would still ask for your promise that you will take the greatest care.'

'I have not forgotten what happened in London. I shall not be so careless again.'

'Then I must leave you. I shall return as soon as possible and I hope to have your brother with me—or at least his blessing.'

'I am sure Andrew will relent when he reads my letter,' Jane said and reached up to kiss him. 'Do not let him change you whatever he says.

Nothing will change my mind. Believe me, I am looking forward to knowing you better and to a future spent together.'

'My dearest one.' George drew away reluctantly. 'I must go or I shall never have the resolve to leave you. Do not forget what I have said.'

Jane promised she would not and stood back, allowing him to leave her. She had told him that she would not allow the thought of Blake to spoil her happiness, but despite her determination, there was a shadow hovering at her shoulder. Her fear was not so much for herself, but for George and her brother. Having met Blake face to face, she suspected that he was even now licking his wounds and planning his revenge. He would not accept his defeat and must be nursing a grudge against the men who in his mind had cheated him of a fortune.

Shivering, Jane went back into the parlour where her godmother was sitting with her needlework. Lady Mary looked up with a smile.

'Lord George has gone, then?'

'Yes, he has promised to return as soon as he can.'

'Do not look so anxious. Lord George has been

in the army. He is well able to take care of himself, dearest. You must try not to think about the dreadful man who had you abducted. Tomorrow we shall start to shop for your trousseau. It is to be my wedding gift to you, my love, and I want you to have all the pretty gowns you could possibly desire.'

'I told you, a wedding is not certain, Godmother. We could both change our minds.'

'Do you wish to withdraw?'

'No, not at all. I think we shall do well together.'

'Then we may safely buy your bride clothes. I am very certain Lord George has no intention of changing his mind. Besides, I want to make you a gift, Jane.'

'Thank you. I am very fortunate to have such a good friend.'

'You must know that you are as a daughter to me,' Lady Mary said. 'I shall rest easier knowing that you are married to a man you love and respect. It is all I have hoped for you.'

Jane smiled and sat down to look at the magazine of fashions that her godmother was offering her. She knew that Lady Mary's words were sound. Lord George was perfectly capable of taking care of himself and she ought not to worry. Yet still the fear remained that he might be in danger.

George was aware that he was being followed. At the start he had wondered if his mind was playing tricks, but he had seen the same man on the same horse at the inn where he had stopped to rest his own horse and eat his meal earlier. That man had been following at a discreet distance for more than an hour since he resumed his journey and it would soon be dark. It was best to face up to the challenge now rather than continue.

He knew that a little farther ahead the bend in the road would hide him from his shadow. He would seize his opportunity to gain the advantage.

Once he was temporarily out of sight, George turned off into the trees and dismounted. He climbed into a tree and watched for the man following him to arrive at the same spot. The road ahead was clear and he should still have been in full view of his tracker. The man's reaction would show whether or not he was actually on George's trail.

Sure enough, the man came into view. His immediate reaction was to halt his horse and look about him. Clearly, he suspected that his quarry had turned off and was deciding which way to go. George leapt down from the tree, grabbing at the man and pulling him down from his horse so that they landed in a heap on the ground together. George was fortunate in coming off best for the man was beneath him, breaking his fall. He lay winded and stared up at George, shocked and resentful.

'What the hell did you do that for?' he muttered as George rose to his feet and allowed him up. 'You might have killed us both.'

'I doubt it. A little tumble from a horse did no one any harm,' George said blithely, dismissing all the bruises and broken limbs such falls might cause. 'I considered it the lesser of two evils, for I did not fancy a ball in the back.'

'Damn it,' the man muttered. 'You were in no danger. I've been protecting your back, my lord.'

'Indeed? Did Price send you?'

'He's the Runner?' The man shook his head. 'I've heard the name, but I don't know him.'

'Then why—and who the devil are you?'

'Stark is the name, my lord. I heard Captain Blake plotting to have you murdered and decided I would stop him if I could. I've been watching you since you left London with the young lady. I trust she has recovered from her ordeal, sir?'

'Yes, she has, little thanks to you, Stark.'

'I made a mistake, my lord—as you did in trusting Blake once. He loaned me money when I needed it and demanded service as repayment. I had little choice, for I would have found myself in debtor's prison had I refused him—or mayhap in a ditch with my throat cut.'

George nodded. 'Miss Lanchester told me that you treated her well, apart from the abduction and deceit you practised on her godmother. I understand you prevented that rascal of a landlord shooting her when she escaped?'

'I couldn't stand by and let her be shot.'

'I am surprised you lived to tell the tale. Blake must have been furious.'

'She was no use to him dead,' Stark said. 'He

cursed Rab for a fool and blamed him for leaving the door unlocked, then went off in a rage, vowing to see you dead and Miss Lanchester's brother ruined. I left before he returned to the inn.'

'To my knowledge he has not yet done so,' George said and frowned. 'Am I to trust you, Stark? How do I know that you are not lying?'

'We have travelled many a mile this day, my lord. I had you within my sight most of the time. Had I wished to put a ball into you, you would even now be dead.'

'Yes, I think I believe you,' George said. 'Do you know where Blake has gone?'

'I might have an idea,' Stark replied. 'He is a man who knows how to blend into the background, sir—and he is a master of disguise, though he cannot change his eyes. What he did to your lady is not the first or last of his crimes. With what I know about him, he would be certain to hang.'

'If you could help put Blake behind bars before he caused more mischief I should be grateful.'

'Would you give me a place in your household,

sir? I do not ask for much—an under-footman would suffice for my needs. I want honest work.'

'Serve me well, and I shall repay you in the way you wish,' George promised. 'I am going to meet Lord Lanchester. Ride with me and tell me what you know of this rogue that we should all like to see punished.'

'I will that, sir, and rightly gladly. He is a rogue and the sooner he meets his fate the better.'

Chapter Eleven

'There is a letter for you,' Lady Mary said, entering the parlour where Jane was sitting with a book. 'It has Lord George's frank. I am certain it is good news and you have been worrying for nothing, dearest.'

'Thank you.' Jane took the note eagerly and broke the wax seal. She read through the first few lines, then looked up with a smile. 'It is good news. George has made up his differences with Andrew. My brother has written to *The Times* newspaper to announce our engagement.' She turned the page. 'Andrew sends his love and says that we should have the wedding at home as soon as we are ready to go ahead. He will join us here in Bath for two days before he returns to his regiment. George says that he has an errand and will be with us by the end of the week—which is three days.'

'We shall have done most of our shopping by then,' Lady Mary said. 'Any work the seamstress has not completed can be sent on. If the wedding is to be held at your home, I believe we should hold a little dance here, my love. This house does not have a room large enough, so I shall go today to see if we can hire one of the public rooms.'

'That would be perfect,' Jane said. 'I would prefer a quiet wedding at home with only our close friends and relatives, but the dance would be a good way of repaying all the kindness and hospitality we have received here, Godmother.'

'That is exactly what I thought,' Lady Mary agreed. 'Does Lord George say what kind of an errand detains him, my love?'

'No, just that he is delayed and will see us at the end of the week.'

Jane was thoughtful as she folded her letter and tucked it into her reticule. Was Lady Mary right in thinking she had been worrying for nothing? A tingling sensation at the nape of her neck was telling her otherwise. Her fiancé had not given her a reason for his errand, but she suspected it might have something to do with Captain Blake.

He had spoken of giving her time to decide if she wished to marry him, but her mind was made up. To be his wife was what she wanted above all else. She could only hope he felt as she did that their wedding should be as soon as possible.

She held her sigh inside, wishing that she was not still haunted by the shadow of her recent abduction. Blake had been so very vindictive. She could not think that he had given up his plans for revenge.

'I am sorry, my lord,' Stark said as they left the seedy inn, which he had told George was the haunt of highwaymen and rogues. 'I know Blake has been involved in dealings with various rogues who frequent the inn. They are a close-mouthed lot, but they know me and if one of them had seen him, they would have told me. I have been given the name of another inn where he might be hiding out. I suggest that you return to Bath to your young lady, sir. I shall continue the search, and if I discover anything, I'll let you know.'

'If you find him, follow him. Keep close, but take care that he does not see you,' George said. 'Send word to me and I will set the Runners on him. I shall not have time myself so I must leave the search to you and others.'

'Am I right in thinking that your wedding has been announced, sir?'

'A notice has been sent to *The Times*. It should appear this weekend. We shall be announcing it to our friends in Bath and then travelling to the country for the wedding. Why do you ask?'

'If Blake hears of the wedding, he may try to do something on the day, sir—or the day before. You should make certain that you have adequate protection for your young lady, in case he tries something.'

'Jane is under surveillance the whole time,' George said, his mouth set in a grim line. 'If anyone tries to harm her, my people have instructions to shoot immediately.'

'I should have known you needed no instruction from me,' Stark said and smiled oddly. 'I'll see if I can discover where Blake is hiding, sir. The sooner he is caught and punished, the better.'

'You know that he might incriminate you?'

'You'll speak up for me, sir?'

'Yes, certainly.'

'Then I'll take my chances.'

'If you have no luck with your new lead, come to Bath. You are a useful man to have, Stark.'

George nodded to his self-appointed bodyguard and they parted company.

Jane returned the books she and Lady Mary had borrowed from the lending library and crossed the road towards the teashop opposite. She wanted to purchase some bon-bons for her godmother and knew that Lady Mary was partial to the marchpane comfits.

Her shopping finished, she walked home at a brisk pace. It had rained earlier in the day and there was a chill in the air, which made her feel she would be glad to be in the house. Lady Mary was giving a dinner that evening and Jane did not wish to be late. She saw that a carriage was driving quite fast down the road she wished to cross and paused at the edge of the pavement, glancing one way and then the other as she waited for it to pass her.

It was as she was about to step into the road that she felt a prickling sensation and glanced behind her. A man was standing a few paces away. He was staring at her and she was certain he had been watching her with his one good eye, the other being covered by a black patch. Normally such an affliction would have roused her sympathy, but there was something about the man that made her nerves jangle with apprehension.

Feeling chilled, Jane ran quickly across the road and knocked at the door of her godmother's house. It was opened to admit her, but she looked back to where the man had stood. He had moved on a little, but she had the feeling he would loiter somewhere and watch the house.

'Is that you, my love?'

Lady Mary came into the hall as Jane took off her pelisse and chip-straw bonnet, handing them to the footman who had admitted her.

'Yes. Have I been ages?' Jane asked, moving towards her. 'I kept meeting people and they all wanted to say hello or wish me happy.'

'Yes, people are amazingly kind. Another three gifts were delivered this morning,' Lady Mary said. 'Your brother has arrived, dearest. He seemed to think that George would be here before him, but it is not so.'

'His letter said the weekend. This is Saturday, but I suppose he might have meant tomorrow.' Jane frowned anxiously as she went into the parlour and saw her brother standing before the fireplace. The housekeeper had thoughtfully lit a fire for them, because the afternoon had turned chilly. 'Andrew—how are you?' Jane greeted her brother and went to kiss his cheek.

'I am perfectly well,' Andrew said and held out his hands, looking into her face as she took them. 'What of you, Jane? I had your letter, but I wanted it from your own lips. You are quite sure this is what you want?'

'Yes, perfectly. I was not certain that I wished to marry, but all my doubts have gone. I love George very much. I do not think I should know what to do if I were to lose him now.'

'He certainly cares for you,' Andrew said and smiled. 'You know my objections—but I shall admit that he *has* redeemed himself. Mariah had nothing but praise for the man who rescued her.'

'She is staying with her friends now, I think?'

'I believe she may have left with them for Italy. There she will be cared for and safe—and should soon recover from her ordeal.'

'I am glad for her sake.'

'As we all are, of course.'

Jane looked at him in silence for a moment. 'Are you smitten, Andrew? Have you fallen in love at last?'

Her brother frowned, then, 'To be honest with you, I do not know, Jane. I feel something—but it may be sympathy. I dare say time may help to clarify my feelings.'

'If I were you I should not leave things there, Andrew. Could you not take an extended leave from your duties, whatever they may be?'

'You think I should follow her to Italy?'

'If you like her enough, I think it might be a good idea—but I must not interfere, Andrew. You are my brother and I should dearly love to see you settled and happy, but only you will know if your heart is engaged.'

'There are things that must be put right before I could marry.' Andrew frowned. 'And must the heart be engaged? Many couples marry for mutual respect and fortune, Jane. Mariah might do well to marry so that she is no longer the target of fortune hunters—but I am not certain of her feelings.'

'That would not do for me. I suspect that you are too like me to be satisfied with such a marriage.'

'Then I shall consider my options—after your wedding,' Andrew said. 'Tell me, dearest sister— what would you most wish for as a wedding gift? I dare say Marlowe has all the silver and linen you will ever need—so something for your personal use, perhaps?'

'You are the fourth person to ask me that question today,' Jane said. 'I was asked twice on my way to the library and once in the teashop.'

'Really?' Andrew's brow creased. 'The engagement can only just have been announced in the papers. Lady Mary must have spread the word.'

'She has many friends here. I dare say she told them in confidence. Everyone is so kind.'

'Yes—but if everyone knows, then Blake must

know, too. George is still concerned about that rogue, though for myself I believe he may have taken himself off abroad. He must surely know there is a warrant for his arrest?'

'Yes, I am certain he would know.' Jane was thoughtful. 'I was followed from the library this afternoon. I saw the man before I returned the books and again before I crossed the road just now. I was wondering—is George having me protected?'

'Yes, of course. Had he not seen to it I should have employed Runners myself. We do not want a repeat of what happened in London, Jane.'

'I thought it must be so,' Jane said, feeling relieved. 'I was a little nervous of the fellow who followed me today. I have caught a glimpse of others, but this one seemed to intend me to notice him and I wondered…' She shook her head. 'No, I shall not imagine things. George will be here later today or tomorrow. Our dance is in three days' time and then we shall go home.'

George glanced over his shoulder. He could see no one, yet he had an uncomfortable feeling that he had been followed for the past hour or so. He had stopped a few miles from Bath to rest his horse and eat his dinner. It was after he left the inn that he had begun to sense he was being followed. Somehow he did not think it was Stark this time and a prickling sensation at his nape told him that whoever the man was, his intention was not good.

George regretted his choice of inn. It was not one he would normally frequent. He ought in truth to have spent the night at the last decent posting inn he had passed, but he wanted to keep his word and reach Bath before Jane retired for the night. However, it was dark now and his shadow would find it easy enough to creep up on him before he knew what was happening. He urged his horse a little faster. The sooner he was in Bath the better.

The shot came from somewhere to his left and passed so close to his cheek that he felt a breeze. Had he not chosen to put his horse to a gallop, it would no doubt have found its mark.

Once again his sixth sense had come to his rescue. George could not be certain that the would-be assassin was in the pay of his enemy. It might just be a thief hoping to pick off an easy victim and rob him, but George's instincts told him that Blake meant business. He was no longer thinking in terms of a ransom, but meant to kill George—and perhaps Andrew and Jane, if he could manage it.

Bending forwards over his horse's neck, George raced through the darkness. He had taken a chance travelling alone, but he would double his efforts to make certain that Jane was protected from Blake's spite.

Jane heard the knocker just as her foot was on the first stair. She halted, turning to look as the footman opened the door. Seeing the man she had longed for, she gave a glad cry and ran to him. George stepped forwards and caught her in his arms, holding her close.

'My dearest,' he said and gazed down at her face. 'Were you so anxious for me?'

'I could not help it. I know you will call me foolish, but I have been on thorns this past hour, thinking something had happened to you. I had almost given up hope of seeing you this night and was on my way to bed.'

'As it happens, someone did take a pot shot at me in the dark,' George told her. He took her hand and kissed it as she gasped. 'You must not worry, my love. I am here safe with you—and I shall be with you now constantly until our wedding. I do not think we need to delay more than the customary three weeks for the banns to be read—do you?'

'I am sure of my mind—if you are?'

'I was never in doubt,' he said and smiled, taking her hand. 'Lady Mary was good enough to offer me a bed until we go to the country. We shall be together all the time, Jane.'

'Yes. I shall enjoy that, George. I know you have had me watched. Why did you travel alone?'

'I trusted my instincts and they served me well twice. The first time I was being watched for my own safety, which is a long story and will keep for tomorrow—the second may have been Blake or simply a rogue looking for someone to rob.'

Jane shivered. 'I wish that man were in prison.

He is evil, George. I think he would kill us all if he had the chance.'

'He shall not have it,' George said, taking her hand firmly and drawing her into the parlour. The candles were burning low, because everyone else had gone up and Jane had lingered until the last. He put his arms about her, holding her pressed against his body. Jane lifted her head for his kiss. 'You mean the world to me, my darling. I do not intend that Blake and his rogues shall spoil our happiness.'

Jane melted into his body, her heart racing as his lips caressed hers. His tongue sought entrance, teasing her as he kissed her deeply, forcing all else from her mind. All she could think of was the sweetness of his kiss and the deep need he had aroused within her. Her body cried out for things of which she had no experience, and she looked up at him with love and desire.

'I can hardly wait for our wedding day. I want to belong to you, to be yours completely.'

'You can be no more impatient than I,' George told her and kissed her forehead, then the tip of her nose and then her lips once more. His hand caressed the nape of her neck, sending shivers of pleasure down her spine. 'I have thought of you constantly, my love. I want to make love to you so much.'

'I want it, too,' she said, her lips parting on a sigh. 'Everyone is in bed. We are alone...'

George gave a husky laugh. 'You have no idea how you tempt me, my darling. Yet I shall not anticipate our wedding. You are innocent and lovely and you would give generously, but I am determined that everything must be perfect for us.' He stroked her cheek, then kissed her once more. 'Go up now, dearest. I shall stay and have a brandy before I seek my own bed.'

'I love you,' Jane said and smiled. 'I am so glad you are here now. Everyone has been asking for you.'

She left him and went back into the hall and up the stairs. Her godmother looked out as she passed the door of her bedchamber.

'Lord George has arrived safe and sound?'

'Yes, Godmother. He is here.'

'I was certain he would be,' Lady Mary said. 'You will sleep soundly now, my love.'

'Yes, I shall,' Jane agreed and smiled.

She would not worry her godmother, though she was certain that Blake had not given up his quest for revenge.

Alone in the parlour, George sipped his brandy as he sat by the dying embers of the fire. The attempt on his life meant that he would have to be on his guard the whole time. An attack was unlikely to take place in Bath in daylight, but at night, on the road to Jane's home—or on the day of the wedding—he would have to double the men protecting them all.

The next morning George accompanied the ladies to the Pump Room to meet and be congratulated by all their friends. After seeing Lady Mary comfortably settled amongst ladies of her own circle, he and Jane went walking together through the streets of Bath. Jane bought an impressive intaglio cameo brooch set in gold for her godmother and George insisted on purchasing a pretty turquoise-and-pearl, heart-shaped pendant on a fine gold chain for Jane.

'You will spoil me,' Jane said. 'I did not bring you here to buy me a present.'

'Would you spoil my pleasure?' he asked, a teasing look in his eyes. 'Am I wedding a scold?'

Jane laughed. 'It is true that you hardly know me, but I promise I shall not scold you—at least not often.'

George laughed out loud. 'Please do not make promises you cannot keep. You have scolded me from the first, my dearest one, and I would not have it different. This is the first time we have been shopping together, though it shall not be the last. I want to share all your pleasures, Jane— and I dare say I shall buy you many gifts on our honeymoon.'

Jane took his arm and they continued to walk along the street, stopping to glance into the windows of the shops they passed, ending by taking coffee and cake in the teashop opposite the library.

Reminded of the previous day, when she had been followed, Jane glanced over her shoulder, but could see no sign of the ruffian who had seemed to stare at her so oddly. She frowned, because the man had looked to be a rough sort and she was not certain he had been one of the Runners George was employing.

However, she decided against voicing her doubts, because they had had such a happy time that morning and she wanted to put the shadows of the past few weeks out of her mind.

'A penny for your thoughts?'

George's teasing words brought her back from her reverie. 'I was just thinking how pleasant this is,' she said. 'I am so very happy, George. I can hardly believe that we shall be together always. I never expected to be so fortunate.'

'I had not considered marriage until I met you,' George said and touched her gloved hand on the table. 'And then, when I understood my heart, I thought you would never forgive me for what I had done.'

'I knew that I owed my freedom—and per- haps my life—to you,' Jane said, looking into his eyes. 'At first I was angry with you, but my anger soon turned to admiration for your courage and resourcefulness. I know that you risked your life for Mariah and for me. Yet even then I was not sure I truly wished for marriage—but then I began to see that without you I should only be half-alive. I know that I would risk anything to share your life, even if we did not have for ever and a day.'

'I would give my life for yours,' George said. 'Without you I should not wish to live.'

'Then we are in perfect agreement,' Jane said. 'Tell me, where are we to live, George? I know you have a fine town house—but shall we live at the country house you took me to that first night?'

'I dare say we may choose to spend some part of the year there. I have had some of the rooms refurbished since then,' George told her. 'The estate was left to me by my great-aunt, but I have another in Sussex. My father's estate is small, but the house is very pleasant. I think we shall go there for a few days before we leave for our honeymoon so that anything you wish changed can be set in hand and ready for our return.'

'Two country estates and a town house.' Jane arched her right eyebrow in a teasing manner. 'Am I marrying a wealthy man?'

'I do not think myself the richest man in England, but we shall go on very comfortably—what makes you ask?'

'When I ran away from Blake that morning, I was lost in a maze of poor streets near the river,' Jane said and a shadow passed across her face. 'The children wore rags. Their feet were bare and their faces were covered in sores. The men had sullen eyes and the women looked as if all hope had gone. If we are rich, George, could we not do something to help the poor in those slums?'

'I sit on the board of two charities for orphan children,' George replied and his look was one of warm approval. 'I am certain that you would be very welcome to join any charity you wished or you could even set up your own, Jane.'

'I shall begin by joining an established board,' Jane said. 'I need to learn about the way things are done, but then I should very much like to set up a charity of our own, George. Something we could take an interest in together.'

'I should be delighted to join you in your venture when you are ready,' he said. 'As my wife you will have an independence of your own and may do as you wish with your own money, but I should certainly contribute and I have generous friends.' He smiled. 'Does that ease your mind a little?'

'Yes, it does. I had not realised how hard life was for some people until that morning, George. I have seen poverty in the country when the mines close or a hard winter means the crops are scarce, but I have never seen anything like those slums.'

'The area you were in is one of the most deprived in London,' George agreed. 'I have heard talk of a slum clearance, but sometimes all that does is to move the problem on, because the people are driven from their homes.'

'New homes must be provided before the houses are pulled down, I think.'

'I agree with you,' George said. He took out his gold pocket watch. 'I believe we should return to the pump rooms now, Jane. Lady Mary will wonder where we are.'

The following days had been spent as pleasantly as the first, Jane discovering day by day how much she liked the man she was to marry.

He was charming, amusing and generous, well liked by everyone. They visited friends, welcomed others who called with wedding gifts and prepared for the dance to celebrate their coming nuptials.

'People are so very kind,' Jane said on the morning of the dance. 'I have received so many gifts today. Most are flowers and bon-bons, little tokens for the dance, but some of the wedding gifts are very generous.'

'That diamond bracelet from Lord and Lady March is very handsome,' George said. 'Lady March is a great friend of my sister, you know.'

'I hope Lord and Lady Markham will come to our wedding, George. I have invited them both.'

'Then I am sure they will. My sister is most eager to get to know you better, Jane.' He hesitated, then, 'You might care to know that she has told her husband everything. He asked about the brooch that was lost and she decided it was best to confess. He had suspected something and was glad it was over. I think they will do better together in the future.'

'I am glad for her sake that she has done so. I

suspected that he knew something the evening I was invited to dine. Her confession will clear the air between them.'

'Had she been brave enough at the start, perhaps none of this business with Blake would have happened.'

'Your sister might then have been his victim. What happened, happened, dearest. It is over and forgotten.'

'It is almost over.'

'Surely he must have given up and gone off abroad by now, do you not think so?'

'I hope so.' He smiled at her. 'If you would care for a drive about town this morning, my love, I am at your service. I have sent for my curricle and the groom will have it ready in an instant. I know you plan to spend the afternoon quietly at home to prepare for this evening, but the day is fine and a short drive would be pleasant.'

'I should like that very much, if you will wait one moment while I run upstairs and put on my bonnet and pelisse?'

'Of course.'

George nodded his approval as she went off,

then turned to Andrew, who had just entered the room.

'I have had a report that Blake was seen here yesterday,' he said. 'I do not think he will dare to try anything in Bath, but we leave the day after tomorrow. It is then that we should be on our guard.'

'You think he will not dare to attempt anything in Bath?' Andrew frowned. 'You have your people watching for him, I know, but the man is sly and may adopt a disguise. Be careful, Marlowe. His pride was mortally wounded when Jane floored him and escaped. For a man of his nature I think that would be more galling than my shot, which merely winged him.'

'I would to God you had killed him,' George said, then lowered his voice as he heard Jane returning. 'Not a word of this to Jane. I do not want her pleasure in the dance to be overshadowed.'

'You need not remind me,' Andrew replied. 'I am truly fond of her, as you know.'

George inclined his head, going into the hall to meet Jane. 'You are lovely as always,' he said. 'That shade of green suits you very well, my love.

I have noticed that you often wear green—is it a favourite?'

'Yes, I do like green,' she said. 'It suits my colouring. What did Andrew have to say?'

'Nothing that need concern us this morning,' George said. 'Just some business. We have an appointment at my lawyer's office this afternoon—just a mere detail to clear up.'

'I see.' Jane took the arm he offered and they went out into the warmth of an exceptionally sunny late August day. 'This is the first time you have taken me in your curricle, George. I should like to drive a rig when we are married. Will you teach me?'

'Yes, certainly,' he agreed. His groom had a very smart curricle with yellow-painted wheels drawn up at the side of the road. George offered his hand to Jane and helped her up, then went round to climb up himself. Just as he was putting his foot to the step someone called out a warning. An instant later a shot rang out, followed instantly by a second.

'George!' Jane cried as the horses shied and one of them reared up. The groom, who was at their head, held on to the reins for dear life and managed to stop them bolting and trampling over the body of the man who lay in the road. 'George, my dearest love.'

Jane hurriedly dismounted and ran round the back of the curricle to where George lay on the road. A moan of distress trembled on her lips as she knelt down and turned him. She could see that the assassin's ball had passed through his coat sleeve and his arm was bleeding. The impact had knocked him down, but he was recovering and opened his eyes, attempting a smile of reassurance.

'It's just a flesh wound. I'll be fine in a moment.' Jane rose and offered her hand just as a man came up to them. He bent down and helped George to his feet, supporting him as he swayed.

'You, sir! Did you shoot my fiancé?'

'No, it is all right,' George said, his face very pale. 'If I am not mistaken, it was this gentleman that shouted a warning and then—did I not hear a second shot?'

'Blake will not be troubling you again, sir,' Stark said grimly. 'I shot to kill. If I had shot first, I should be guilty of murder. I am sorry you were hurt, but I tried to warn you, sir. I was not sure he meant to fire until that moment. He has been following Miss Lanchester and your good self for days. You had the note I sent you earlier?'

'Yes, I did,' George said. 'I shall…'

Whatever he meant to say was lost as he gave a slight moan and fainted. Jane cried out in distress, but Andrew had come out of the house and rushed to help Stark support George into the hall. Glancing behind her, Jane saw that two men were bending over a body on the ground at the far side of the street. A small crowd of onlookers had begun to gather and some were looking at her curiously. She hastily followed George and her brother into the house. It was most unfortunate, but the tale would be everywhere by the end of the day.

'I'll go for the doctor,' Stark said once they had George sitting on the daybed in the parlour. 'I'd best go to the magistrate as well and report Blake's death.'

'Leave that to us,' George said, coming out of his swoon in time to hear what was said. 'We'll see to this, Stark. If you tell them you killed a man, they will put you in prison and ask questions later. It may be best if you fetch the doctor and return with him. You should be on hand to answer questions. Andrew, you go to the magistrate and tell him what happened here. Stark undoubtedly saved Jane's life, for had Blake disposed of me, he might have finished the job by killing her.'

'Lie still while I look at your wound,' Jane said. 'I think your coat is ruined, George. You will not mind if I slit the sleeve? The doctor may not come at once and I think we should bind your arm for the moment.'

'It is deuced painful. I believe the ball may be lodged in my arm after all,' George said and leaned back against the cushions. 'Forgive me, Jane. I am so sorry to have ruined your dance.'

'Foolish man,' she scolded and fetched her scissors from her sewing box. Slitting the sleeve of his coat and his shirt, she saw the neat hole where the bullet had pierced the flesh of his arm. Blood was still oozing, but slowly. There was no corresponding hole at the other side, which seemed to confirm that he was right and the ball was lodged in the fleshy part of his upper arm. 'I fear the surgeon will have to cut for the ball. We should perhaps get you to bed before Mr Stark goes for the doctor.'

'Damn it,' George muttered, looking very white. 'I do not think I shall be able to attend the dance this evening, Jane.'

'We shall cancel it,' she said. 'Please do not worry, my dearest love. I care only for your pain—and I am so grateful that Blake's aim was not true, for I am sure he meant to kill you.'

'Mercy on us,' Lady Mary said, coming into the parlour at that moment. 'There is a small crowd across the road, Jane. I dare say the constable has been fetched. I was upstairs and did not hear what happened.'

'Blake tried to kill George and Mr Stark killed him,' Jane said. 'I fear we must disappoint our friends this evening, Godmother.'

'No, please do not cancel,' George said. 'If I am able, I shall make an appearance, but the dance must go ahead.'

'First things first,' Lady Mary said. 'I'll have

the footmen assist you to bed, sir. Once the doctor has been and we know you are in no danger, we shall discuss what ought to be done.'

'I shall go for the magistrate,' Andrew said. 'The sooner this business is finished and done, the better. For myself, I can only say that I am heartily glad Stark shot to kill. We can stop worrying every time Jane goes out of the house.'

Stark and Andrew took their leave. Lady Mary summoned two footmen, who, being large, strong men, carried George up the stairs to his bedchamber despite his protests. A maid had prepared the bed, pulling the covers back. The unpleasant experience had left George a little faint, but once propped up against a pile of feather pillows, he recovered enough to smile at Jane and tell her not to worry.

Lady Mary brought a bowl of cool water. Blood was wiped away and George's arm bound to the ladies' satisfaction.

'I shall bring you up a tisane,' Lady Mary said. 'Please try to rest, sir. I am sure the doctor will not be too long in coming.'

'You are very kind, ma'am.'

Jane turned to leave, but George caught her by the wrist, holding her.

'Please do not go,' he said. 'Sit here and talk to me until the doctor comes. I am sorry that you had to witness such a distressing incident, Jane. I had hoped we might prevent this, but I was not expecting it to happen in broad daylight in the middle of Bath.'

'No, I dare say not,' she said. 'I am not sure, but I think Blake had been following me even before you returned to Bath. He was wearing a disguise, but he looked different from the men you set to protect me.'

George took her hand. 'It is over now, Jane. You must try to forget all this unpleasantness. Put it from your mind.'

'I am not distressed, George. I am anxious for your sake, but the rest is already forgotten.'

'Sure?'

'It is over. The shadow has passed and as soon as you are well again, we shall be married. We shall forget this ever happened.'

'Indeed, we shall,' he agreed and kissed her hand. 'Do you have any idea how very much I adore you, my darling? I wish for nothing more than to claim my lovely bride.'

'You cannot long for our wedding night more than I, my very dearest George. My feelings towards you are quite shameless. I am afraid I am not at all the modest bride I ought to be, for I do not in the least fear becoming your wife in every way.'

'You are lovely in every way and I want you so much.'

Jane bent down to kiss him softly on the lips. 'You must rest, my dearest. I know you are in pain.'

'I shall be better after some sleep. Now promise me you will let Andrew take you to the dance this evening and make my apologies.'

'Is that truly what you wish?'

'Yes, it is. I shall rest and sleep the better for knowing that you have not disappointed all our friends.'

'Then I shall go for a short time. Lady Mary will stay to the last to entertain our friends, but I shall return after the first few dances.'

'You must stay until supper,' George said.

'Now, be a good girl and promise me—and I promise to rest and get well for our wedding.'

'Very well, since you wish it.' Jane smiled as she bent to kiss his lips. 'I shall stay long enough to please everyone and then I shall come home.'

Chapter Twelve

'Are you sure you feel able to travel?' Jane asked anxiously. 'You promised me you would rest and I think to travel after just two days in bed may be too much for you, my love.'

'As I recall, you promised to stay at the dance for supper, but came home after dancing only three times.' George sent her a challenging look. 'I have rested for two days and think I can manage to be conveyed in a carriage. I have no intention of riding my horse at this stage. Besides, I would be at your home this weekend to hear the banns read. I wish for no delay to our wedding plans.'

'I stayed at the dance long enough to receive the kind wishes of our friends and give your apologies, George. Everyone understood and accepted that we had done what we thought best, but I am sure they would have thought me heartless had I danced the night away while you lay sick in bed.'

'I was not fatally wounded, merely in some dis-comfort,' George replied with a twinkle in his eye. 'However, we shall not quarrel, for it is far too tiring, my love. You must consider my state and humour me, Jane.'

'You, sir, are a tease,' Jane replied and laughed. 'I can see there will be no living with you if you do not have your way, but you must promise to rest as soon as we are home.'

'Yes, I dare say I shall have no choice,' George said. He hesitated, then, 'I promised Stark a place in my household. I have decided to make him my agent for the estate in Sussex. You will have no objection, Jane? I know what he did—if the idea upsets you, I shall find him something else-where.'

'He saved our lives, George. Had Mr Stark not killed Blake he would have fired again, at you and me. Besides, he behaved with respect even when he kidnapped me and I believe everyone is entitled to a second chance.'

'You are very forgiving,' George kissed her hand. 'I think I am a fortune man to have found you, my love.'

'We are both lucky,' she said. 'We had best not keep the horses standing for we have a long day ahead of us.'

The journey was accomplished without incident, though George had been pale and quiet in the later part of the first day. He had gone straight to his room without complaint and Stark had taken him up his dinner on a tray and then had dressed his wound, proving himself an excellent valet. The next morning George had been refreshed and they had continued their journey, arriving just in time for tea on the second day.

This time George was feeling able to meet the servants, who had known Jane all her life, and to receive their good wishes. He took tea with them in the small parlour, then retired at Jane's insistence and was given supper in his own room.

By the next morning George's arm was not as stiff as it had been and he was almost back to his old self. He came down just before noon and after nuncheon they spent a pleasant hour or two walking in the garden.

Jane showed him some of her favourite plants. They discovered that they shared a passion for rare and delicate species, and some time was spent discussing the gardens they might build together at their future homes.

It was as they returned to the house that they saw a gentleman walking towards them.

'Good afternoon, Miss Lanchester—Marlowe, I trust you are recovering from your wound?'

'Avonlea, it is good to see you,' George said and offered his hand. 'I am much better, thank you. We shall not need to delay the wedding.'

'I am delighted to hear it. I wish you both good fortune and much happiness.'

'Thank you, sir,' Jane replied. 'How is Lucinda?'

'Very well, thank you. And I have had a letter from Mariah, giving her destination in Italy. She asked if you might think of visiting her this winter.'

'I believe I shall be otherwise engaged, sir. As

you know, I am to marry Lord George. However, I think my brother may wish to travel.'

'Lucinda thought he might,' the duke said and smiled. 'If Mariah could be settled happily, both my wife and I would be very happy.'

'As should I,' Jane agreed. 'If you leave me her destination, I shall write to Mariah and tell her of my wedding.'

'You look very beautiful, Jane,' her brother said as she came down the stairs on the morning of her wedding. 'Marlowe is a very lucky man.'

'I think I am the fortunate one.'

Jane's smile lit her face, making her beautiful. Her gown was of a warm cream silk trimmed with lace of a coffee tone. Her satin slippers were dyed to match the lace and her bonnet of satin was tied with ribbons of a matching shade. Around her throat she wore three strands of creamy pearls fastened with a large emerald-and-diamond clasp. She wore pearl drops on her ears and an emerald-and-diamond bracelet on her arm.

'Marlowe has certainly been generous with his gifts,' Andrew said. The earrings had been his own gift, together with some pieces of furniture, silver and glass that had been their mother's, which he knew meant a great deal to Jane.

'He is always generous,' Jane replied with a smile. 'But I was not speaking of gifts, Andrew. George is brave, kind, witty and caring. I do not think I could have chosen better.'

'As a matter of fact, neither do I,' Andrew replied, surprising her.

'Thank you.' Jane reached up to kiss his cheek. 'That is the best present you could have given me, dearest Andrew. Your approval means more to me than anything.'

'Well, I am glad to have settled things,' Andrew said, a slight colour in his cheeks. 'I have taken your advice, Jane. I intend to travel for a while—and then I may settle down here.'

Jane studied his face and smiled. 'I do not know why you have hesitated, but you should go to Italy,' she said. 'If you love Mariah, ask her to marry you, Andrew. Unless you ask, you will never know.'

'Yes, that is my thought on the matter,' he agreed

and looked pleased. 'And now we had best leave, for we do not wish to keep George waiting.'

'I am so happy,' Jane said as she came out of church to the sound of bells pealing, her hand upon her husband's arm. 'It seemed as if a shadow hung over us for so long, George, but now the sun is shining and we are free to be happy.'

'Yes, we shall be happy,' he said and leaned forwards to kiss her lightly on the lips.

A cheer went up from the crowd of villagers waiting to see the bride and groom leave the church. Children came forwards with gifts of flowers and a straw doll, which was a country tradition said to ensure fertility. Jane took it and then threw her own posy of flowers, which was caught by a young village girl who giggled and looked shyly at a young man in the crowd. Jane wished her luck. Then George took Jane's hand and they were showered with confetti as they ran towards the carriage.

Once inside, George leaned forwards to kiss Jane on the lips. This time his kiss was neither light nor brief, his tongue meeting hers in a delicious twirl of sensual delight that promised much.

Jane was breathing heavily when she drew away, her cheeks a little warm as she gazed into his eyes and saw the passion there.

'I love you so much,' he said huskily. 'I have scarce known how to wait these past weeks. You grow lovelier every day, Jane.'

'Do I?' she asked, oddly shy. Her heart was racing and she longed to be in his arms once more, but the carriage was slowing and they had to greet their servants who had waited at home to prepare the reception. 'I love you more than I can say, George dearest.'

The door of the carriage was opened and the steps let down. George jumped out and gave his hand to Jane, then, when she was on the step, he swept her up in his arms and carried her past the watching eyes and into the house. The family servants clapped in approval and laughed as he set her down and then kissed her full on the mouth in full view of the entire household.

Their love was so evident and everyone felt privileged to share in their happiness, the smiles

and laughter rippling through the watching re-
tainers.

'May you always be as happy as you are today,
my lord—my lady.' Andrew's housekeeper came
bustling up to them, her face wreathed in smiles.
'We all want to give you our best wishes, Lady
Marlowe. It has been a privilege to serve you—
and we hope you will visit with us sometimes.'

'Thank you, I shall,' Jane said, feeling a warm
glow inside. She took George's hand and went
into the huge room that had been prepared for the
reception. Flowers were everywhere and the air
smelled of the delicate sweet perfume of roses.

They stood just inside the door, greeting their
guests as they arrived back from the church.
Everyone had been so generous, and, in another
reception room, the lavish gifts were set out on
a long table for the guests to admire.

The Duke of Avonlea was one of the last guests
to arrive. He shook George's hand, then came to
Jane.

'You look beautiful, Lady Marlowe,' he said
and kissed her hand. 'I must wish you happiness…' He lowered his voice. 'Lucinda was not

quite well enough to attend, but she sent you her best wishes and told me that she wishes to give a dance for you when you return from your honeymoon. She should then be delivered from her confinement and we shall be entertaining again.'

Jane thanked him and he went off to talk to Andrew. She knew that her brother had messages to take to Mariah when they met in Italy.

Jane's heart swelled with pleasure as she circulated through the large room, greeting and thanking her guests. She was excited and happy, laughing and talking, enjoying the pleasures of the day.

George's arm was now fully recovered and they performed a waltz together when the dancing began. After that some of his friends begged for a dance with the bride and she was laughingly passed from one to the other until George put his foot down and reclaimed her.

'How much longer does this go on?' he asked, looking down at her with such longing that Jane laughed. 'Much as I love all our friends, I want to be alone with you.'

'We shall leave very soon now,' she promised. 'I shall say goodbye to my godmother and brother—then I shall go up to change. You may have the carriage brought round in half an hour.'

'I am too impatient,' he said. 'You were enjoying yourself. We shall stay another hour and then you may go up.'

'I am ready now,' Jane told him. 'Say your own farewells, George dearest. I shall not keep you waiting long.'

'How lovely this house is,' Jane cried as she first saw the soft red of faded bricks and the low sloping roof of dark slate. Roses were growing up the walls and she thought their smell would perfume the house when the windows were opened. 'It is one of the prettiest buildings I have ever seen.'

'It is not as large as my other property, but it was my father's house and his before him,' George told her. He stood holding her hand, as they looked at the house in the afternoon sunlight. They had spent their wedding night at a house George had borrowed from a friend, breaking their journey. 'I am glad you like it, Jane. If you listen carefully, you can hear the sea. The cove is just beyond that wooded rise.'

'Is it a private cove?' Jane looked at him in surprise. 'Can we go and look—is it far?'

'Not too far,' he said and smiled, offering his hand. 'We must say hello to our people first, Jane.'

George took her hand and led her to the line of waiting servants, introducing the butler and housekeeper, and then each and every one of the maids, footmen and even the boot boy. He needed no prompting to recall all their names and Jane saw that he was respected and liked by his people, most of whom had been with the family for years.

George swept her up and carried her over the threshold. He kissed her and then set her down, before taking her hand to lead her up the wide staircase.

'These are your rooms, my lady,' he said, taking her through a pair of double doors at the far end of the corridor. 'I hope the décor is to your taste, but if not you must change it as you will.'

Jane looked about her. The sitting room had clearly been refurbished very recently in shades of green and cream. The furniture was satinwood, delicate and pretty and crafted, if she was not mistaken, in Mr Sheraton's workrooms.

'This is so beautiful, and the décor is exactly to my taste.' Jane looked up at him with pleasure. 'Is that why you asked my favourite colour?'

'One of the reasons,' he agreed and took her hand, drawing her into the adjoining bedchamber. The walls were decorated with a pale duck's-egg-blue silk paper and the ceiling had a frieze of plaster flowers and leaves, painted in pale pink and green; the large bed was of mahogany with four posts with delicate reeded carving and covered with a quilt of padded satin. The magnificent tallboy and the chests each side of the bed were of polished mahogany and the writing desk before the bow window had a green-leather top tooled with gold. The elbow chair set before it had a green-striped silk seat. It was set with silver accoutrements and a vase of red roses.

'Beautiful,' Jane said. She glanced around the room, looking for a door. 'Where do you sleep?'

'Here, most of the time, I hope,' George said, giving her a look that made her heart race as she remembered his passionate loving of the previous night. 'But my rooms are through here.'

He opened a door that led into a dressing room and through to a bedchamber at the other side. Looking round, Jane saw that the walls were covered with a bluish-green silk paper and the hangings were also green and cream, touched here and there with gilt; all the furnishings were also of dark mahogany and might have been examples of Mr Chippendale's work.

'Yes, I can see you here,' Jane said and moved towards him, putting her arms about his waist and gazing up into his eyes. 'You have made a beautiful home for us, George. I shall be so happy living here—and the garden looks perfect for our children.'

'How many shall we have? A boy for you and a girl for me?'

Jane gurgled with laughter as she leaned into him, offering her lips for his kiss. 'As many as God sends us,' she said. 'I want your babies, my love, as I want you.'

George cupped her buttocks with his hands, holding her pressed against him so that she felt the heat and hardness of his bulging manhood. Her arms were about his neck as they kissed, their tongues tangling in the sweet dance that made her melt with longing. She pressed closer, wanting to be his once more.

'Careful, my lady,' he murmured hoarsely. 'Much more of this and you will find yourself waiting for your tea.'

'That would never do,' Jane said with a provocative glance. 'What would the servants think if we did not go down to the parlour, but stayed here instead?'

'I'm damned if I care,' George said and swept her off her feet, carrying her to the bed. 'You are a minx, Lady Marlowe, and I think I need to give you a lesson in how to behave.'

'Yes, my lord, I think you do,' Jane said and smiled as he took off her shoes and tossed them to the ground. 'I cannot wait to begin my lessons.'

Afterword

Andrew stood at the window of his study, looking out at the night sky. Jane's wedding was over; she had left on her honeymoon and all the guests had gone. It was strange how empty his house felt. He had never expected that he would miss his sister this much or feel so alone.

How ridiculous! He might have married years ago had he wished, but, after a first calf-love that ended in bitter regret, Andrew had not thought of marriage. His relationship with his sister had been close for many years, and he'd put his disappointment from his mind, making a life in the army for himself and leaving the estate to Jane.

He had left the army because of a distasteful incident that had left him feeling disillusioned with the behaviour of fellow officers. Andrew's own behaviour had been exemplary, but the disgrace of some of his friends had left a shadow. The death of an officer, the rape and murder of an officer's wife in circumstances that had never been fully explained, had left a nasty taste in his mouth. He had planned to put the incident behind him and make a life on his estate, perhaps marry.

His feelings for Lucinda had been strong and, had she been free, he might have asked her to marry him. However, she was Avonlea's wife and very much in love with him. Mariah Fanshawe had always been around when he was a youth and he had not taken much notice of her when she returned to Avonlea after she was widowed, until she shot the rogue who had blackmailed and then tried to murder Lucinda Avonlea. He had felt admiration for her coolness and quick thinking, and become aware that she was no longer a spoiled girl, but a very beautiful and exciting woman.

He'd known that Mariah was flirting with him in the weeks following that incident, but he had not been certain of his feelings for her. Admiration for her spirit, yes, and an awareness of her beauty and her exotic perfume, the way she carried herself and her pride. It was her pride that had made him stop and think. Mariah was brave, but she was also reckless and inclined to believe that she could have her own way whenever she wished. Andrew had wondered if their personalities were too alike for a comfortable marriage and so he'd hesitated—and then he'd heard of the rumours circulating.

He had thought the scandal of the dead officer and the officer's wife had been settled, but now it seemed there was some doubt. Accusations were flying back and forth and even Andrew's own name had come into the affair.

He was innocent of any wrongdoing, but he had been involved. He had known something that he did not declare at the original court inquiry. His commanding officer had believed him completely, but there was still a mystery. A mystery that Andrew had pledged himself to solve.

A man's good name was in jeopardy. Unless Andrew could help him clear his name he might be court-martialled and, if found guilty, hung for murder—and Andrew could be accused of being an accessory to the crime.

How could Andrew ask any woman to marry him with something of that nature hanging over him? After Mariah's abduction he had been torn with grief and the realisation that she meant more to him than he'd imagined. Jane had advised him to ask Mariah to marry him—but supposing he was unable to get to the bottom of the old scandal?

Nothing could be proved against him, but the accusation might be there—and if it were generally known the scandal would be unpleasant.

Andrew intended to travel to Italy and give Mariah the letters entrusted to him. However, there was another reason for his journey. He must trace a man who had once been his best friend, a man who had disappeared after his wife was raped and murdered.

Until he found Laurence, Andrew would not have time to investigate his own feelings for Mariah. Was he truly in love with her—or had he merely been concerned for a young and lovely woman who had been so cruelly abducted?

He grimaced as he turned and went upstairs to instruct his valet to pack. Only time would reveal the answers to all the things he needed to know.

* * * * *